THE **C**ROW WHO
         TAMPERED
         WITH
         TIME

HUMDINGER

Humdinger: A striking or extraordinary person or thing.

IN THE ORIENT A REST was the dear Old Briar-patch, near the Laughing Brook and the Smiling Pool, lived the wonderful bunch of characters of Thornton W. Burgess's books, which our teacher began reading to us in the first grade. Sammy Jay, Unc' Billy Possum, Shadow the Weasel, Chatterer the Red Squirrel, Prickly Porky and the rest contended with each other's nasty ways, getting into remarkably human scrapes and adventures while steering clear of Farmer Brown's boy and his dog, Bowser the Hound. When my daughter and her chicken gave me *The Adventures of Jimmy Skunk* for my birthday one year, the whole cast came popping up from the pages and from a long-neglected corner of my mind.

One late fall day in Diefenbaker Park, I was startled by a little critter as it emerged from a gopher hole — ears round like Mickey Mouse's, face like a small lion's peering from above a curiously long neck. It took off in another hole, stood for moments, sneaked in and out of the bush, and away with bulbous black-tipped tail flying behind.

THE CROW WHO TAMPERED WITH TIME

LLOYD RATZLAFF

thistledown press

© Lloyd Ratzlaff, 2002
All rights reserved

No part of this publication may be reproduced or transmitted in any form or by any means, graphic, electronic or mechanical, including photocopying, recording, or any information storage and retrieval system, without permission in writing from the publisher. Requests for photocopying of any part of this book shall be directed in writing to CanCopy, 1 Yonge Street, Suite 1900, Toronto, Ontario, M5E 1E5.

Canadian Cataloguing in Publication Data

Ratzlaff, Lloyd, 1946–
The crow who tampered with time

ISBN 1-894345-43-6
I. Title.
PS8585.A853C76 2002   C818'.603   C2002-910321-5
PR9199.4.R37C76 2002

Cover triptych detail: *Split Decision* by Andre Petterson
Book and cover design by Jackie Forrie
Author photo by Larraine Ratzlaff
Typeset by Thistledown Press Ltd.
Printed and bound in Canada by AGMV Marquis

Thistledown Press Ltd.
633 Main Street
Saskatoon, Saskatchewan
S7H 0J8

Thistledown Press gratefully acknowledges the financial assistance of the Canada Council for the Arts, the Saskatchewan Arts Board, and the Government of Canada through the Book Publishing Industry Development Program for its publishing program.

ACKNOWLEDGEMENTS

I made every reasonable effort to obtain permission to use copyrighted material. Thanks to Random House Group Ltd. for letting me quote from D. T. Suzuki's *Living by Zen*, published by Rider.

Earlier versions of some of these pieces appeared in *Forefront*, *Guidelines*, *Journal of Mennonite Studies*, *Kaleidoscope*, *NeWest Review*, *Prairie Messenger*, *Quest*, *Rhubarb*, and *Spring*; and in the Transitions anthology *Where Your Life Stories*. Many of them celebrate Saskatoon's Diefenbaker Park. I thank the Chief for lending his name to this place, and for two cases of Diefenbaker meat when I was a kid — some families got four, so we weren't as poor as I thought.

CONTENTS

Prologue: Being Here   9

A

The Bush on the Grave   12
Vixats   16
An Unexpected Fox   22
How Not to Scare a Gopher   28
The Crow Who Tampered With Time   33
The Sound of One Cow Grazing   37
Humdinger   42
The Holy Crow   45
The Why and the Wherefore   47

B

Of Bulls and Baptisms   52
Archangels and Jingle Bells   61
No Biscuit Blues   65
Sweat   74
The Barrier of the Patriarchs   77
O Wheel   80

C

Willy Becker and the South Church	84
A Medicine Story	93
Two Fathers, A Half-dozen Moths	97
Der Schoener Mann	102

D

The Champion	108
Harry Ziegler's Philosophy	122
Beginner's Mind	126
Silent Night	129

Epilogue: The Sound of a Going — 132

For Larraine

PROLOGUE

BEING HERE

*O*scar Wilde once said that if faced with a choice between going to heaven or going to a lecture about heaven, most people would go to the lecture. We seem to be suspicious of a paradise in a far-off time and never-never land — some professing to believe it, some wishing to believe it, others believing it's unbelievable. How different all this is from Thomas Traherne's experience: "Your enjoyment of the world is never right, till every morning you awake in Heaven; see yourself in God's palace; and look upon the skies, the earth, and the air as Celestial Joys; having such a reverend esteem of all, as if you were among the Angels."

Love and work: these were Freud's criteria of a successful life, the reasons for staying on this planet at all. Yet both can be degraded from opportunity to opportunism, and both can come to feel like joyless obligations. Are compassion and creativity better terms? Are we here to experience common passion, and to make something of the experience? It's one way of phrasing the spiritual quest.

The first thing Christ said when he began teaching was, Change your mind — the realm of heaven is at hand; and

Norman O. Brown elaborates, every passing minute brings it no closer. Our appointment with life is in the present moment; yet most of us are like the student who kept pestering the Zen master, Where do we go when we die? until the teacher slapped him and said, One world at a time!

I no longer make New-Year's resolutions. I know how feeble willpower is. I make only these daily resolves: to breathe consciously; to smile as often as possible; to give up worrying; to accept the present moment with reborn attention. Year-end and year-beginning are fictional times separated by no more than a breath or the blink of an eye. In that breath, in that blink, eternity resides.

Lost in time, we look for directions to get away. Here in eternity we love and we work.

a

THE BUSH ON THE GRAVE

*I*N THE PIONEER CEMETERY beside Diefenbaker Park near my home in Saskatoon, there is a grave on which a chokecherry bush is growing, hanging heavily some autumns with ripe black fruit. Vandals often desecrate other graves in that place, but as far as I know, they've never damaged this one. Beside the South Saskatchewan River, in the middle of a patch of prairie, in the centre of a grave, the bush stands over the remains of a little boy named Vernon Leo Kuhn, who lived in this world for six months in 1902 and 1903. It's the only bush of its kind in the cemetery. I have often thought that, if it were done respectfully, those dangling clusters of cherries could be made into a unique wine. But no one ever seems to pick them; perhaps people are too superstitious to do it, or perhaps some fluke of nature allows them to ripen there until a person such as I comes along, ripe himself for the kind of experience which befell me there one afternoon of the first of September.

I don't say I would have felt free to pick those chokecherries if I had intended simply to make a drinking wine. For wine and its related spirits have sometimes caused me more trouble than they were worth; but when I set out for the cemetery with a plastic pail in the late afternoon sun, I pondered the untidy leave I had taken of my family's Christian fundamentalism — affirming the leave-taking, but regretting the pain — and hoped for a sacramental wine to come of my day's endeavour.

I passed through a clump of poplars bordering the cemetery, where a magpie jabbered at it knew what, and stepped onto prairie grass toward the little plot where a century ago an infant was lowered into the earth by its grieving relatives, and shovelled over, and left to the straying forms of life which would overtake that parcel of ground. Winds would blow, animals would forage, seeds would fall, and one of them would strike roots toward the child. One day the navel of the earth would open, and a plant would come up and turn into this bush, which so many years later had produced the cherries before which I stood with my pail.

The chokecherries will become wine, will become me — Vernon Leo Kuhn will become me. So arrested was I by this thought, that I sat down before the weathered tombstone to commune with the child. My tradition's sense of the sacramental had been so sparse, its means of grace so subjective and elusive.

"I don't know," I said to Vernon Leo, "how it is that you were here for such a short time, but I want to tell you that a tree has come from your body. There was a seed which found you with its roots, and the roots took you up into the air, into a bush, with some help from the light and wind and water from the sky. And the cherries on it, little boy, are wonderfully sweet; I know that, because the other day I tasted them, and now I'm going to pick them to make some wine."

Here I was required to make a promise; the choke in the cherries wasn't lost on me. "I've done some foolish things,"

I said, "with some other wines, but this one will be different. This is your lifeblood, and I wish it to become mine."

A gate opened. I saw all things existing by virtue of consuming and being consumed; I saw that this is how things are, and how the world is therefore the body of God. In the autumnal light I got up to pick chokecherries, and they rolled from the branches through my fingers, funnelling through cupped hands into the pail hanging at my belt. For once, my hands, not my head, did the picking. When my head picks chokecherries, branches are broken, leaves are torn, fruit is squashed; this time my hands knew what to do, though my mind reminded me that later I would crush those cherries to a bloody pulp and trample them like Yahweh in his winepress.

"I Am," I said to the bush, uncertainly at first, then more boldly, "I am the I AM-ness." And with that, I had broken through the sometimes-despairing, sometimes-defiant sound of it, to the name of God: I AM what I am — that is my name for all time, by which I shall be invoked for all generations to come. The Jewish text and the Christian eucharist echoed a Zen monk's joy: "I eat food, I am food!"

My death ceased to matter. I was able to say I AM and not require that it refer to myself, or not only to myself. Or it did matter — to creatures who fly and burrow and creep and swim, or who stand growing in one spot, who surrender their lives when I eat them; who, when the translation of all languages is done, also say I AM, as I do. For an hour I picked chokecherries, while the world was one round mellowness within and around, and tenderness and clarity and trust. I was Caleb, weighted with vintage from the promised land; or I was John Donne in heaven, where it is always autumn, for things are ever at their maturity.

The mystics have always been confident that we don't have to go anywhere, for I AM is where we are — at this bush with the baby and the cherries, in the city with its impetuous horns and lonely terrors. Vernon Leo Kuhn never imagined himself as a human ego with a name, never emerged far enough to confuse himself with some lost and disconnected thing which only we — and we falsely — had supposed him to be. We are lower-case i's; but Vernon Leo stayed nearly enough I AM for that pestiferous ego never to have taken shape, and he of the scarcely-sexual body didn't have to travel nearly so far back as the rest of us.

Mother Julian of Norwich said, "I was shown no hell harder than sin." We puzzle and fret and fight over our straying from the communion we once knew, and sin becomes a strange word as it becomes a familiar experience. And repentance, that other strange word, means: How could I have forgotten? Thank God, now I remember.

A dead child under a chokecherry bush. Sweet wine.

VIXATS

*J*OE AND I WERE PICKING HAZELNUTS one afternoon in southern Manitoba twenty-five years ago, when a little animal startled us as it scurried off through the bush. We had startled *it*, I suppose, and Joe chuckled in Low German at "that little *Vixat*" as it left us for parts unknown.

"What's a *Vixat*?" I asked.

Joe thought awhile and said, "It's something that appears suddenly."

But he seemed hesitant, so I probed. It didn't mean this or that animal, he said after another pause, or necessarily an animal at all. If an unexpected thing pops up, it's a *Vixat*. The popping-upness is what makes it one.

Joe and I were born Mennonites, but where Low German was his mother tongue, mine was a corrupt High German spoken in deference to my Lutheran grandfather who had converted after falling in love with the daughter of a South Dakota Mennonite minister. Grandpa never spoke more than a dozen words of English or *Plautdietsch*, and *Vixats* were not among the phenomena we recognized. I'm sorry that my tradition sacrificed the vivid diction of Low German to the rantings of frontier revivalism. We became so preoccupied with going to heaven that we never noticed, for instance, that a vacuum cleaner is really a *Juehlbassem* — a howling broom — or that a locomotive is an *Iesehinxt* — an iron stallion. Joe taught me these things long after I left home.

Yesterday I saw eight *Vixats*. I had been reading a batch of final exams from students on the eve of graduating with their teaching degrees. They had been the most unmotivated, unreliable, uninspired class I had encountered in twenty-odd years at the university. They hadn't found it possible, for instance, to attend classes frequently, or submit work on time, or write anything that didn't make me want to fidget, scratch, or yawn. Adolescent psychology wasn't my favourite subject anyway, and I was glad to be done with these students who seemed hardly past adolescence themselves. What remained was to read their exams, and as I read I recalled a cartoon of a woman selecting a graduation card for her loved one. The shelf was in two sections: GRADUATION (Literate) and GRADUATION (Illiterate).

I read, I scratched. I looked through the window at a spring day dawning after a cruel and protracted prairie winter. University deadlines nagged. Diefenbaker Park and the South Saskatchewan River beyond the window tempted me severely toward a walk. I gave in.

Along the path I began thinking of trinities — body, mind, and spirit; ice, water, and mist; father, son, and holy ghost. I can't help it, I'm one of the creatures who does this sort of thing. I imagined how I was one with the native woman and the steel-cabled jock in the class, how two people and a god make one marriage, how my dead father and my living mother are myself, how the soul is a midterm, airier than body but more gravid than spirit. Suddenly a *Vixat* sprang and two others followed before I came to a halt. Three souls danced above the path, trinity in motion, psyche, soul, and butterfly — and around the bend came two bicyclists pedalling hard in fashionable gear and scattering the souls to the wind.

I sat down in the wake of their velocity, hoping to lure the others back, those who had been transformed from heavy worms into near-spirits, who had left so swiftly at the approach of unseeing humans. I lay flat on the path to persuade them I wasn't wicked, and when one fluttered back I extended a hand, the *Vixat* touched it and flew off, and William Blake and spring's first butterfly and I were another trinity kissing the flying joy.

I should have stayed longer, but the old disease of impatience drove me to my feet, and by the time I got to the railway bridge I was fussing over adolescence again. I needed another *Vixat* — and earth's smallest gopher sprang from nowhere and streaked toward a hole and vanished downward as I swayed again in my tracks. Of the million gophers I've seen on the prairies, none was half as fast as this little dash of chirping light who shook me with laughter and caused the exams to disappear again.

I've never heard of anyone who actually paid a fine for walking on railway tracks. Still, the law provides that nothing else shall go where trains go. Roy Romanow himself was once scolded by the CN for standing on their tracks in a television re-election commercial, and when a reporter asked for his comment, he could scarcely find words. He managed only to say, "If those corporate so-and-sos are worried about safety, why don't they send a few trains along this track?"

I have often sat there and waved at the *Iesehinxts* going by. I've chatted with workers repairing rails who didn't seem to think I was a threat to the transportation industry. Now I trespassed again and tried to balance on the rails. I do this occasionally to assess my age. I can't perform the way I used to, but if I can do it at all I don't feel old. I fell off, of course — I was forty years and forty pounds past adolescence. I stepped up and balanced again, toppled to left and right, got back on track, and the hugest garter snake slithered into the grass and threw me from the rails, and I heard Joe saying *Doa foat vada 'n Vixat* — There goes another popping-up thing disappearing. I have walked around Diefenbaker Park easily a thousand times in fifteen years, and never seen a snake of any size; now this reptile appears to a jaded lecturer on a day he particularly needs inspiration — how does that happen?

Don Juan used to say to Castaneda, That crow you saw wasn't really a crow. That puff of wind you felt wasn't wind. That shadow was actually an Entity. That man over there isn't a man, it's an Ally beckoning. He engineered shock after shock to Castaneda's conceptual system — sometimes "reluctantly" with the aid of his power plants — to rid the scholar of the fatigued labels he had hung on all the world's things to avoid new-ness and perpetuate his old self-ness; and the crow became an Omen, the gnat Something Else when it bit, the wind a Spirit as it struck. A sorcerer jars mystery back into experience, and a *Vixat* by definition comes from nowhere.

I turned from the tracks into the grass where the Entity had vanished, skirted a mud puddle, edged by another bush toward the road leading home to the exams. A strange sound! Something like a chirp, a bit like a warble, perhaps a kind of whistle — but mostly like nothing I knew at all. It was a Power and it made me listen.

Another critter in the grass, I thought, and tried to locate it. But the sound came from above, from a power pole. Two woodpeckers hung there, heads tilting back, necks thrusting vigorously left and right, uttering sounds into the sky while I stood below for the fourth time startled past my exams. The woodpeckers seduced each other, and abruptly fell silent and looked over the prairie, then danced again hanging on the pole. When one sang, the other sang; when one looked around, the other looked around; when one turned a throat to the sky and sounded, the other had followed before I could register it.

I craned my neck until a kink made me feel the pain as well as the joy of seeing. The woodpeckers moved around the pole; I circled to bring them back into view, and one flew off in the direction of my home while the other left for a bush on yonder side of the tracks. I apologized as they went: I didn't mean to spoil that thing you were doing.

Where the dirt road turns to pavement, there is a little swamp in which blackbirds live when they come to Saskatoon. I was just beginning to fume about the exams again when something called from among the swamp's twisted sticks. I wished for a red-winged blackbird, but the sound remained hidden. I threw a stone, and when the something flew away silently, I saw an ordinary blackbird without red wings.

Saw? When you *see*, Don Juan said, there are no longer familiar features in the world; everything has never happened before. He was an old man when Castaneda first met him (or invented him, as some say), long past the temptation to use his sorcery for egotistical ends. He wanted the scholar to be a pupil again, to see an ordinary bug or a customary shadow again for the first time. It's more exciting not to know which bush the rabbit is hiding behind, he said, than to act as though we know everything — a gentle philosophy, occasionally requiring harsh means for its conveyance. Once a magical deer talked to Don Juan. On hearing this, Castaneda was cynical as usual and asked what the deer had said. The sorcerer claimed it spoke like this: *Hello, friend. Why are you crying? Don't be sad* — words rather too ordinary for our egos, until we hear them again for the first time, in which case they are magic.

Those butterflies had been heavy and dead for a long time; then they danced in the air. The gopher said I was going too fast, like the bicyclists, but he could go faster. The snake sang slip sliding away. The woodpeckers made love under these living prairie skies, and said I should stop thinking that a Mennonite can't learn to dance — although I'd like to discuss this further with them. And the black-winged blackbird left the swamp saying, Man, you are a slow learner.

The world is a *Vixat*. But I am full of exams.

AN UNEXPECTED FOX

I am not the first man to have lost his way only to find, if not a gate, a mysterious hole in a hedge that a child would know at once led to some other dimension at the world's end. Such passageways exist, or man would not be here. Not for nothing did Santayana once contend that life is a movement from the forgotten into the unexpected.

— Loren Eiseley

IN HIS ESSAY COLLECTION *The Star Thrower*, Loren Eiseley told of an encounter with a fox pup one morning beside an abandoned boat on a beach, just as the sun was coming up. He had sat all night under the open sky, dozing and dreaming and thinking about his departed father. He didn't know that the decaying hulk of the boat against which he was leaning was a fox den. But at sunrise a little creature crawled out and showed him a miracle, he said, which cured him of the common sickness of gazing with upright human arrogance on the things of this world.

The pup inspected him carefully, then offered him a chicken bone between its teeth. On a childlike impulse, Eiseley — esteemed scholar that he was — went down on all fours and picked up another bone in his teeth, and shook his head vigorously in reply. With that the two creatures tumbled to the ground and played, and there Eiseley had his miracle. It was very small, he said, as is the way of great things; but, he concluded pensively, "there is no use reporting it to the Royal Society."

Once upon a time the prairie village where I grew up was full of gates and holes into other dimensions. Now in my middle age it offered only distressed and beggarly sights. Uniform government housing on windswept acres stood where, in my childhood, hovels of miscellaneous shapes had squatted among crooked hedges and untended shrubs. The old railway station had been burned down years ago by kids playing with matches, and the occasional trains that came through afterwards begrudged their stops at its remaindered platform, until the track was torn out entirely and the trains were free to go elsewhere. The skating rink had been sacrificed to a bulking new arena with L-A-I-R-D lettered loudly on its roof. The old hill behind the schoolhouse was nearly sawed in half from snowmobiles going up one side of it and down the other, where once upon a time a snowmobile meant a huge Montreal Bombardier driving over white winter fields, delivering supplies to the village when nothing else could get through. And the concession shack on the sportsgrounds where I hazarded my first smoke was long gone.

This is not how the village is supposed to look.

I was visiting my parents one day, who still lived there in a new prefabricated house. I rarely went home without ritually faring through every street in the village, to remind myself of what used to be there and lament what I found in its place. I finished my visit and exposed myself again to the grimness of my threatened hometown, and drove off to where I knew things were better.

The valley toward which I headed lay along the bank of the North Saskatchewan River ten miles distant. My roots were there as much as in the village; there my ancestors had toiled, and played and prayed, and the land was still in the family, worked now by a younger cousin who had taken a happy leave of academia after his ninth grade. Something kept calling me back. Though I had often heard how lucky I was to have escaped the unbearable poverty of the thirties, still I felt cheated not to have encountered the power of this place in its elemental days. For years I escaped my urban conveniences to return to this river valley, to feel what was left of its old spirit. The abandoned trail winding down the hillside beckoned me to follow its eroded and overgrown contours, until I reached the second bend where the land and water first came into view, where my childhood eyes drank in a serene sight and most of me always came home.

That summer afternoon I sat on the ground against a boulder my grandfather had pulled under the maples to ease the cultivation of the land before me, which my eyes now scanned for the ten-thousandth time. Here I had played as a child while our elders told stories at family gatherings, while the chokecherries ripened around us, and across the wheatfield the timeless river flowed by.

A rusted Overland car body still lay in the bushes nearby, as it had for more than forty years. Long ago I pushed aside the underbrush to look at it lying there, with fears of forsakenness weighing on my childish mind, and today its abandonment still seemed a solemn thing. Behind me rose a steep hill from whose summit I had often looked over the valley, imagining the hundreds of bison skulls my grandfather's plow turned up when he broke the land, skulls which had lain through uncounted seasons since the aboriginals drove the animals over the brow of the hill in their hunts. Only little stones were left now, washed down in many springtimes by the creek which gurgled and swam from the hill. And over there stood the mud-plastered house and log barn where my parents had lived before I was born, both buildings leaning with age, empty shells through whose holes I could see the river beyond. And rising on the other side were the green hills which in my young years had seemed so exotic, which bordered a strange and forbidding country where the race of Doukhobors lived. I knew nothing about them but that their name sounded ominous: Doukhobors.

But this side of the river was mine. Its stones and bushes, its hills and springs and trails awakened old mysteries, drawing me through their gates and holes into Wonderland. Off to the right leaned a weather-beaten gatepost as old as I was, its bark dry and curled, barbed wires twisting aimlessly about its aged knuckles . . .

On the other side of the gate a little fox came running, swerving along the trail and darting into the wheatfield just as some people hurtled round a bend in the distance. They were chasing the fox, and they'd lost him. It wasn't uncommon these days for strangers to come down to the family's river flat, and I wasn't surprised so much as annoyed at their intrusion. I didn't like those people, I didn't want them bothering that little animal, and without hesitation I sprang up and ran into the field where a motion in the grain betrayed the fox's direction.

"Lie down!" a voice urged; "lie down and think small."

I fell to my hands and knees and still seemed very bulky. I lay prone on my stomach, and began shrinking. Green stalks rose above me and stretched into a forest, and there I was, looking for an animal of my own size, while far away some human beasts lumbered unseeingly by.

Then he was there, sniffing over dampish ground, ears erect and a right paw poised tentatively in midair as he spied me. I wondered dimly whether he'd bite, but reached out to pet him in spite of myself, and in another instant we were tumbling on the ground and playing with abandon among the towering trees.

I tired out soon and called for a rest. Stretched on the earth with the fox pressing at my back, I began drifting toward sleep. I supposed he'd be gone when I woke; but then, I hardly knew where I'd take him anyway.

Consciousness dawned again, and a movement behind me jolted me back to the forest. The fox was still there, and when he began sauntering through the wheat toward the old house, there was nothing for me to do but follow. I think you will laugh when I tell you he talked to me; but talk to me he did, and I to him. I can't say what he said — a dream fox doesn't speak like a human who thinks he's awake — but we gossiped amiably and long as we strolled. It was not a newsworthy event. I'm not certain it was a literary event; but that day a little fox was pleased to gossip with me in my ancestral place. Gossip, I learned later, is the Old English *godsibb*, kinship with a god.

Call it a dream, then, or a dream within a dream. It doesn't cancel the experience, which itself cancels the boundaries between lives normally imagined to be inimical to each other. Once upon a time I returned to Eden, and its fox and I were friends. Then a great divide reinserted itself between the dimensions, and I couldn't haul him across, and I have no idea where he's gone.

Very well. In this world he'd only be hounded by tabloid photographers, or scorned as something pertaining to a half-lunatic Lloyd who himself hobbles so clumsily through this two-legged adult world. But St. Augustine said of one of his own returns to innocence, "The world may laugh at me for this, and while it laughs I shall feel sorry for it." Wonderland isn't as far away as we think. Little beings wait there for us to shrink to childsize, and to play — or for that matter fight — according to less troubled rules than those which govern us here.

We hurry by the gateways in our business of bending the world to our own proportions. Wonderland is everywhere, and we refuse to be small.

HOW NOT TO SCARE A GOPHER

GAY BALFOUR IN CORTEZ, COLORADO WAS HARD UP. He worked at a marina but was looking for ways to raise extra cash, when one night he had a dream. A huge yellow truck fitted with green hoses drove through a cornfield at five-hundred miles per hour, vacuuming prairie dogs from their holes. And when he woke up, he resolved to build such a machine. He went shopping for a street sweeper, modified its workings, and looked further for suitable hoses to attach. In a certain industrial supply shop a clerk pointed at some bright green flexible tubing, and a chill went through Gay Balfour: he had seen hoses just like that in the dream.

He dubbed his machine the "DogGone", claiming it could vacuum twenty acres, or eight-hundred holes, on a good day. It sucked gophers from the ground and deposited them, alive but somewhat bewildered, in the back of the truck to be "relocated" — heavy artillery in farmers' war against gophers, which promised to eliminate the need for the poisons that had been used to date. But how many of the confused animals had been relocated anywhere but to heaven, he didn't say.

Our *Star Phoenix* printed this story on its front page, and a few days later another front-page story announced, *Attention Saskatchewan Gophers: Your Days Are Numbered*. It seems a firm in our city was thunderstruck by Balfour's invention, and contacted him at once to inquire about prices. For $350,000 the inventor was willing to sell the DogGone, name and working prototype together, and our firm prophesied a lucrative business here, where so much of our sixty-five million acres of farmland is infested with these little varmints.

One summer day the city felt too close for my liking, and I set out for a walk in Diefenbaker Park. My neighbour's white cat sat expectantly at the door. Well, the park could wait a bit. I settled on the stoop and took time to make the animal purr. It was easy; it took less than half a minute. She even wagged her tail like a dog, and rubbed and rolled and played, and I was ready to go long before she was ready to let me.

Go slowly, I said to myself as I went toward the park, go deliberately. Not because middle age forces you to slow down, but because time is for the taking, which is its point — it offers itself everlastingly for use, it wants to be taken advantage of. Don't go like the French foreign legion: When in doubt, gallop. Do what you want, want what you're doing.

Who said if he could live his life over, he'd eat more ice cream rather than less, would go barefoot earlier in spring and stay that way till later in fall? *Take the shoes from your feet*, I recalled, and complied.

Going barefoot slows you down. It helps to tame time. You *feel* the grass instead of trampling it on your way elsewhere.

When you go slowly you smell the flowers, listen to the bees, hear how mightily birds chirp, see, for once, the diamond sparkles on the river. You can't get to heaven by hurry, only by slow and by stop. So I made my way to a grassy spot above the river and sat down to meditate, to see whether I could bring time to a full stop, and start it fresh again.

This is not easy. My mind, at any rate, is a grasshopper vaulting from here to there, lighting on random stalks of memory and prospect and chewing them over, and jumping to the next and the next, until sometimes the whole doggone field is wasted. I sat that way at first, though the sun shone affably on my face and a small breeze played around my closed eyes. The first minutes are the longest when you meditate, when thoughts are the most obstreperous; but presently I found they weren't running away with me as much as before, though too often I still ran away after them. A few more minutes, as clock time goes, and the thoughts became scarce and spacious, and then I had them instead of them having me.

Sometimes it's tempting to stay in that realm, where thoughts are only occasional visitors; but then again Creation is congenial, too, this world where cats can be made to wag their tails like dogs, where blues and greens are profoundly blue and green when you open your eyes after having closed them awhile. That's what I was anticipating, whenever I should feel like looking again — that unjaded instant when the world's colours flood through cleansed doors of perception — and this was a thought which, for a change, I relished.

I opened. There, about as far as this page is from your eyes, sat a surpassingly fat gopher looking straight into mine. It was a gopher such as I, born and bred on the prairies, had never seen before. I hadn't moved in about twenty minutes, and when he chanced upon me he must have thought I had grown overnight like a magic mushroom. Then I knew: this is not a wild animal, I am a wild animal, and it's my thoughts which make me so. Thoughts are the flaming angel's sword, the only barrier between paradise and me. Relax, trust — this too is a way of having faith.

I waited till the gopher went his way, and I went mine.

A year passed. One warm day, walking near the railway bridge, I stopped when I spied one of these little fellows at the edge of some tall grass beside the bench where I wanted to sit. I wondered whether I could get there without scaring him away, and watch him awhile. (I say him, but in truth I have a completely untutored eye for gopher anatomy.)

I paused long where I stood, and he was vigilance incarnate, motionless on his hind legs, paws protruding under a twitching nose, eyes fastened steadily on me. We played a waiting game, the gopher and I, and he decidedly outwaited me. Eventually I took a barely-perceptible step forward, and waited; another step, and we waited. So I millimetred my way to the bench. It took about ten minutes, but I made it and he hadn't moved. Now we were so close that if I had bent forward and reached out, I could have touched him.

I had a much harder time than he did sitting still. I soon came to a new depth of sympathy for Huck Finn's torment in the darkness of Widow Douglas's garden, when he itched in upward of a thousand places but dasn't scratch because Nigger Jim was a-laying for him a few feet away. Then in a flash the gopher turned, and in another flash had resumed his lookout. Another wait. He grabbed something to eat, stood and consumed it and watched me again; nabbed something at the edge of the grass, and ate with eyes fixed on me.

But what's this! After a half-dozen such dartings, he turned his back and began poking through the grass. I wasn't a wild animal after all — and now he foraged to his heart's content, with long and longer intermissions in his surveillance. And thank God, now I was free to fidget a bit, and scratch my nose, and soon things were very agreeable there above the river, me counting species of birds and he rummaging in the undergrowth.

Then came the most disarming moment of all, when the little guy was overtaken by the wish for a nap. He stretched out at my feet, drowsing in the sunshine with belly upturned, as trusting as could be and as safe as I knew he really was. It had taken about half an hour for him to have faith.

Good luck to you, Mr. Balfour and Company. Maybe you'll do big business with your gargantuan vacuum cleaner, and then will come to pass a new thing under the sun: a prairie without prairie dogs.

Or were you planning to colonize some other planet with them?

THE CROW
WHO TAMPERED WITH TIME

*T*HANK GOD IT'S FRIDAY, we said, and after work headed, as Long John Baldry sang on the stereo, "straightway for the bar." There we disposed of our usual agenda: reviewed the institutional lunacies-of-the-week and illustrated them liberally with anecdotes; fantasized our forthcoming vacations; damned the political process; lamented the nation's — and our own — economic ills while laying out good money for another pitcher of draft; exchanged the jokes which human rights litigation had rendered too hazardous to tell on the job. And eventually we made our ways home to our assorted amusements. An archetypal Friday, it was.

The evening passed with simple diversions, my mind clutching at the weekend's tentative freedom while staving off thoughts of the bygone week or the approaching Monday. Dinner, movies, popcorn, that sort of thing — and eventually it was bedtime.

Count it among life's little treasures: regardless of when you go to bed on Friday night, *it doesn't matter*. Glance at the clock if you like — it only enhances the smugness with which you retire, promises to let you wake up as and when you will, defers to another clock embedded somewhere among the biology you put to rest. Ah, the weekend has begun.

There is no measure of passing time in the depths of sleep, and I didn't know how long I had been away when something reached across the dimensions and began stirring me vaguely toward consciousness. The dim whatever-it-was gathered itself into definition: visitor and butler at once, a crow outside the window announced himself, and simultaneously the dawn of Saturday. I muttered something about why we say a crow caws and a rooster crows, and pulled the quilt over my ears. He announced himself again. In the bedroom an evil eye opened and looked at the clock. It said 7:30 a.m. and I said a bad word in reply. I had every intention of sleeping till noon, while the crow began making clear his intention of prohibiting it.

For a few minutes there was this cycle: downward through silence I drifted back toward sleep, up to the day the crow cawed me; silence and downward drift, cawing and upward summons. It went on until I threw back the covers and groped toward my housecoat, scowling over my shoulder where through the window I saw the offender perched on a power pole looking out over a Saskatoon summer morning. And cawing again.

On the way to the door my mind cast about for a rock to hurl at the crow, along with a curse to make him regret whatever impulse had set him so close to my window. But an angry aura must have preceded me, for I hadn't opened the front door of the apartment when I saw him fly off toward Diefenbaker Park. I grumbled my way back to bed and, somewhat more fitfully than hoped, fell back to sleep;

but when I woke again, it was close enough to noon for me to claim victory.

Saturday passed as Saturdays will, and Saturday night. Bedtime came, and again I was pleased not to set the alarm. Eventually waves of drowsiness were there, and the drifting . . .

. . . and I heard it again — that vaguely familiar something intruding from a remote universe into my weekend nirvana. The crow, the bloody crow again. I looked at the clock. 8:30 a.m., it said, and I praised God I had at least been allowed to sleep an hour later than yesterday. I wouldn't wait so long this time, tormenting myself with hopes he'd leave on his own; I'd go outside at once and cast the stone at him. But after a few loud reminders that he, too, was a child of the universe with rights to be here, he flew away of his own accord, and presently I sank back again into the regions of sleep.

But soon he was back. The infernal cawing began again, and the same contrary pull out from a deep delicious place toward the bleakness of a weekend now nearly spent — and that unrepentant crow asserting his position there on top of the world. Now I *will* get that stone, I said, opening my eyes on the clock . . . and found myself face to face with a display that read 8:00 a.m.

I rolled over in surrender. The crow went away to return nevermore, and I went, foiled and chastened, back to sleep.

I am not writing fiction here. One weekend there was a crow who shifted the boundaries of my reality by tampering with time, and to this day I have no way of knowing whether it was the first or the second awakening which was the dream, or whether both were, or neither was. The digits on the clock glowed as truly red the one time as the other;

the bedroom furnishings stood as substantially at one moment as at the other; my conviction of being awake was as self-evident the first time as the second.

As Sunday afternoon declined toward evening, and evening toward blue Monday, that crow began to seem like an emissary from beyond, a grating angel whose loud squawks cracked open one reality to startle me awake to another. What was the time, really? And if a crow's caw can bend time around and make it run backwards, can show you it's not the time you think it is, who is to say the colleagues and kids, the cabbages and kings around you now cannot stop time in its tracks and reveal themselves as herald angels? Then it becomes possible, after all, to say thank God it's Monday; thank goodness it's now.

That, at least, is what I think the crow said.

THE SOUND
OF ONE COW GRAZING

I KNOW A GOOD PLACE. By day I tramp around its trails and through its bushes, stoop like one of Gideon's failed soldiers to drink water at its creek, gaze at things that flap and fly there, and listen to others that chirp or shriek or thump. Sometimes I talk to these creatures as if we were all children, and sometimes they reply.

But when the sun sinks below the hills across the river, stillness pervades and the dark closes in, lively critters withdraw to their thickets and nests and holes, and I am alone. There are no conveniences and no diversions — no television, no music, no toilet but an outhouse huddled in a distant black clump of trees: and if I don't take a bottle of brandy with me, no insulation of any kind against the vastness and silence.

Here I become a boy again. In daylight, adventures beckon: spreading trees are familiar spirits, no creature fails to announce the world's wonders. But when the place goes dark, the spooks driven off by city lights congregate, and if I'm alone I hear them, too.

Five generations of my family have known this place. My old people used to see aboriginals dragging their travois across the other end of the valley, and here my grandfather's plow unearthed the skulls of the bison which the natives had hunted. My parents lived here before I was born, and when they moved to a less lonely place uphill, they continued farming the land while I played here through childhood's slow days. Later I worked with them, lending adolescent strength to the hauling of stumps and stones so our wheat could grow beside the river. Most of my youthful memories are daytime images of springs and coverts, and the ancient river, and fabulous wild things like the bats we roused from the vacant house by beating on its crumbling walls.

I'm past fifty now, and I still go there in quest of magic. Once in awhile I stay overnight — to scare myself, to conjure another kind of enchantment, the shuddering and creeping and knowing again that vastness contains all manner of things. Something in me wonders where the wonder has gone, and the place pulls me back.

My marriage of nearly twenty years expired. She wished for the old-time religion, while I (as I supposed) was far along in recovering from it. My ten-year vocation as a clergyman ended with the separation. I feared for my ten- and twelve-year old daughters; a legion of inward demons sneered about wretchedness and guilt, and I learned something about the blues I hadn't known before. Often I fled the city to visit my ancestral place, invoking its sunshine and calm, pursuing childgone paths through old terrain, sitting long and vacantly on big rocks, imploring the land to restore some innocence amid the rubble of fallen dreams. But when evenings came I hastened back to the city, to its lights and crowds, to a bar where one night an old black musician said, "The blues is just a good man feelin' bad," and man, I knew what he meant.

One day I made up my mind to stay at the river, and for once encounter the night, to peel off some insulations and feel the place alone in the dark. I wish I could say I had taken nothing but a blanket with me for warmth, like a hopeful elder seeking a vision; but that evening I parked a trailer under a bent maple tree which had felt friendly since my childhood, and sat beside an old stone firepit.

A breeze floated from the hills behind me and along the creekbed, roaming its way toward the river. A few clouds hung on the horizon as the sun went down, and white wisps overhead patched themselves into a gray blanket between land and stars. Songbirds fell silent, busy drones ceased, poplar leaves waited. While I could still see, I went scavenging for sticks and branches and dragged them thankfully to my stone circle, and lighted a light.

And I sipped some brandy, a little medication against the elemental things. I had ways of justifying the insulations. The Christ in whose name my life was steeped had refused even a swallow from the wine-soaked sponge fetched up to him, in his anguish, at the end of an olive stick; but I wasn't him. And who was I, then?

I sat with thoughts about children and church, marriage and ministry, the world and its women. From time to time, something made me venture out toward a dimly-divined circumference between the camp and the night. I didn't know where the edge was, I only knew I was getting close when the spooks began threatening, and then I hurried back to the fire.

Hours passed. Finally I rolled the logs over, stared at the pulsing embers until they dimmed, and retired to the camper. I pulled the curtains across the windows to shut out the night, and sat in the glow of a little kerosene lantern. And I wrote. About Adam eating forbidden fruit and dragging Eve from the garden; about a little cage full of the Bible; about the patriarch Jacob fighting with a demon which really was a God, and limping away in the morning as a different man. The lantern's light reached toward the corners of the camper, and I felt less alone.

Long after midnight I blew out the flame and crawled into bed. Good night world and women, good night children and church. Now I lay me down to sleep.

During the night something came. I heard it through a shroud of sleep, advancing slowly and beginning to circle. As waking widened to a crawling skin, and eyes to saucers and a mind to huge imaginings, I heard that it was a throat. It breathed the way a throat breathes when no human voice orders it. It circled in the night so far from the city, voicing itself at the border of two worlds and coming into this one. Jesus, I prayed, and God and Mother help, while somewhere another old bluesman sang *You can call on your mother, but your mother cain't do you no good.* I lay fending off the sound, admitting it, exorcising, listening again. I had wanted something, and now it was here. It breathed another circle, circumference closing in, deep-throated spook an octave below the blues, circling too slowly and tearing something as it went breathing in the night. At the boundary between worlds, time is a fiction stretching on forever or packing half a life into minutes. Alone and with frail insulations, there is no choice about listening.

Finally I crept to a window and peeped under the curtain. A black shape loomed there, raised its horns slowly toward the window. The beast had broken through a fence and wandered along a cloudy night into the patch of grass around my camper. She had not come to terrify. She was eating grass, and making milk to soften somebody's cornflakes for breakfast in the city, so they could be strong to do what city people do, until they land exhausted in a blues bar, or are driven down to the river to build a little circle of comfort, which turns out to have no power whatsoever against the sound of one cow grazing.

Jacob craves forgiveness with a craving as selfish as the original sin. The angel is just an angel, going its way by day or by night.

HUMDINGER

Humdinger: A striking or extraordinary person or thing.

*I*N THE GREEN FOREST and the dear Old Briar patch, near the Laughing Brook and the Smiling Pool, lived the wonderful bunch of characters of Thornton W. Burgess's books, which our teacher began reading to us in the first grade. Sammy Jay, Unc' Billy Possum, Shadow the Weasel, Chatterer the Red Squirrel, Prickly Porky and the rest contended with each other's nasty ways, getting into remarkably human scrapes and adventures while steering clear of Farmer Brown's boy and his dog, Bowser the Hound. When my daughter and her children gave me *The Adventures of Jimmy Skunk* for my birthday one year, the whole cast came popping up from the pages and from a long-overlooked corner of my mind.

One late fall day in Diefenbaker Park, I was startled by a little critter as it emerged from a gopher hole — ears round like Mickey Mouse's, face like a tiny lion's peering from above a curiously long neck. It took off for another hole, stood for an instant, snaked in and out of the earth, ran again with bulbous black-tipped tail flying behind, vanished into the next hole, and appeared again from the ground.

For once, I had remembered to bring my binoculars with me. I sat down in the grassy triangle away from the road, and tried to bring him closer. Sometimes he was just a blur. Then again he stopped, slipped down and up, dashed further and did it again; and before long we were a merry-go-round, I with my binoculars twirling at the centre, he running and rooting at the circumference.

After a dozen revolutions he crossed the road. I went after him and sat on a stubby fencepost, and focused the binoculars again. His business brought him ever closer, until he was at arm's length, and I laid the glasses down and looked at him eyeball to eyeball. I was tempted to try to touch him, but recalled an earlier unsuccessful attempt to communicate with a wild gander, and left it to this humdinger to prescribe the terms of our acquaintance.

He went about his affairs and let me watch him for an hour, and for that hour I was a child again, although a child probably would not announce to the air of the park, as I did, "I love this world, I love being here" — a religious ejaculation owing entirely to Shadow the Weasel, for I had concluded that the humdinger was none other than he.

How could I have lived fifty years on the prairie and never seen a weasel?

Two elderly men approached on one of their twice-weekly rounds of exercise in my park, one of them labouring heavily on his cane. I waved at them to come — Oh look! oh see! — but they had already spotted him, and he with the cane said gruffly, "That little bastard, he's a survivor." The other added, "He's death to gophers, that's for sure."

They told me what they knew about him. For one thing, that he wasn't hunting just then, only locating the gophers. "He don't have to store up food," one said, "he'll come and get 'em in winter — he'll be white by then."

"He's a little mapmaker," I said.

I suppose he is white now. So white that I've never seen him again, though I keep looking for a little black bulb going over the snow in the park. Shadow the Weasel is one of the ways in which the world keeps me, as Lewis Thomas said, permanently startled. Once someone asked me what I'd write about when I had lost my sense of wonder. I didn't think then to say, "That might be a good time to die."

Consider the weasel of the field, how he weasels. He don't store up food in bins, though plainly he has a certain sense of tomorrow, and heaven sees to his feeding. It's not a good saying for gophers. But for another humdinger who frets about tomorrow and next month and retirement portfolios, what to eat and drink and wear, it's just fine.

And meeting Shadow that day resurrected a ditty we used to sing at recess back when our teacher read us those first-grade tales: *A penny for a spool of thread, a penny for a needle, that's the way the money goes — Pop! goes the weasel.*

THE HOLY CROW

A MURDER OF CROWS is occupying the bush across the street. At the moment, three of them are perched on a power standard looking through crows' eyes simultaneously up and down the South Saskatchewan River, while the rest squall harshly from the bush. What malign intent they have I can't say, but my neighbour, Mr. Black, counted twenty-two of them; so it's not a bunch of crows, or a flock or multitude of crows, but a murder.

One of their ancestors killed me over there in the pioneer cemetery a few years ago. I was walking one evening full of lethal thoughts toward somebody in Ontario whom I had never met, who had done something with someone that I didn't want him to have done. A few minutes earlier I had been sitting in a grove of trees in Diefenbaker Park, communing with an edenic world — steel blue glint of sunlight on the wings of a magpie, patient bumbling of bees from flower to flower, the rumble of the train on the trestle filling the dome of the world — when all at once I was in a ferocious fight with an imaginary enemy. And I fought harder as I began realizing that something in me was wrecking the communion. I strode through the cemetery, a jealous buffoon with enough sense to know

I was doing wrong but not enough to stop doing it. Meanwhile, the world had not gone anywhere; it waited, as always, to be inhabited with presence.

At that instant a crow flapped angrily overhead, beating the air about my ears, hoarsely delivering itself of an oracle as it flew toward the river, and I started to laugh. As the peace had been jarred to pieces by the jealousy, now that abomination was shattered by a crow, and a jealous fool went down with it.

So paradise is lost and regained, so I am damned and saved. Grace makes me laugh at my scrimmages on Creation, trying to make everything more like what I think I want. Grace is also a durable freedom, even to become a snake in the garden.

Begin with communion. Then stray carelessly, willfully, addictively. We have been in paradise and have managed to get out, and we can certainly find a way back in. Let jumbled images and crazy thought-trains go forever through malignant worlds — at any time crow-gods can shout in our ears, lines from books and bibles halt the craziness, tunes from the Bayou Swamp Band direct us back to communion. And when a jealous devil is dead, unaccountably there is Billy Bray going his way, left foot saying Glory and right foot saying Amen.

The kingdom of heaven is like a man walking in Diefenbaker Park, with a heart full of hate and a mind full of venom. Therefore God sends a crow to cry into his ears saying, Wake up!

Across the street the crows from the bush have flown up to join the others on the power pole. They sound agitated. But I ask not for whom the crows caw; they caw for me.

THE WHY AND THE WHEREFORE

Eeyore stood by himself in a thistly corner of the forest . . . and thought about things. Sometimes he thought sadly to himself, "Why?" and sometimes he thought, "Wherefore?" and sometimes he thought, "Inasmuch as which?" — and sometimes he didn't quite know what he was thinking about.

— A. A. Milne

CINDY IS AN EIGHTEEN-YEAR-OLD STUDENT of Larraine's who is inclined to deal with everything in her world by one comprehensive explanation: "That's why because."

Some people call her mentally disadvantaged. Larraine co-ordinates her educational program, and living with Larraine entitles me to a debriefing at the end of every working day where she needs to tell, and I need to hear, stories about annoyingly innocent people.

"I'm going home on the bus today, that's why because," Cindy says.

"I got new shoes yesterday, that's why because."

Things are as they are, because they are.

She is closer to the truth, probably, than we are. For explanation lies on us like a disease in which we forfeit our sense of wonder — the curiosity that drives the best kinds of science, and the humility which is close kin to worship. "How marvellous this is!" said an old Zen saint; "I chop wood, I draw water." One day when my daughter Sheri was five, colouring a picture, she said, "No wonder you like green!" "Why is that?" I asked, and she said, "Because it has such a nice colour."

Less explanation, more exclamation, and we might be spared the embarrassing lengths to which we sometimes go to explain ourselves away.

Suppose the point of Creation were to be able to look at the world and say the divine words: Behold, it is very good. What if we no longer saw bits of stuff strung causally through space across time, saw all things rather as the eternal kenosis of an endless mystery? When you drink water, think of its source, a Chinese proverb instructs — not this cistern or that raincloud or some distant mountain peak, but the Source, which is what *surges*. Creation surges up, that's why because.

I sit under a tree in Diefenbaker Park. Long branches form a canopy over my head from a seed unfolding around me, and this makes me a believer. A little germ upthrusting and downreaching and outspreading, feeding on earth, air, fire, and water; water flowing up to branches as well as down to roots, the tree finding levity as effortless as gravity — and do I know why it surges? In this little cosmos, an axis branches toward the light of upper air, and roots itself into dark dirt below. A centre fashions itself a trunk big and tough, to stand here with complete absence of boisterousness; *why* is not half so transfixing as *that* it's doing so at all. Forty years ago, when I was a kid travelling toward Saskatoon from my village fantasizing about the toys in Adilman's store, this tree stood surging here; and unless developers come with machines to demolish it, it will stand here long after my eyeballs have become a rat's liver. That's why because.

This tree sometimes hears my confessions. It stands massively tranquil while I fret, shelters me as I slow the frantic flash of myself into the patience it already knows how to be. I've read that when Kalahari Bushmen kill an animal for food, they don't thank their idea of God for it, they thank the animal. Just so, I thank this tree when it pulls me toward the Source.

One night in a television documentary I saw Joan of Arc's magic tree, and other trees where "pagan" rites were held, and ancient hills and pools where an unbordered Presence brooded in silence. I felt how these ageless places abide the coming and going of generations, how one is alone there in a silence having nothing to do with the details of anyone's biography, alone with the repository of the last secret. These ancient haunts, these perduring hills and trees, these immense times and the littleness of my life, and oh my children . . .

I crawl out from under the tree and walk to the river. I spread a blanket on a favourite patch of grass above the bank and lay my bookbag beside me. Then I sit and wait.

Many visitors come and go: anonymous flying insects, robin redbreasts, black bugs, the shrieking gulls and the perpetual crows. There's a wondrous hebraic phrasing in the Greek text of the Book of Revelation, where St. John heard "harpers harping on their harps." On the river down there I see a flotilla of honkers honking their honks.

A slow enchantment begins. I say hello to the callers as they arrive, and goodbye when they leave. It's only on the surface that we speak different languages. I will not molest these friends, for I do not consent to Adam's fall. I can't explain this world, but by God it surges, that's why because.

On a blade of grass a bug shines in the sun, crawls a little way along, turns and poises for takeoff — then it's there on the other blade; it flies at the speed of light, dematerializes here and reappears simultaneously over there. Every bug and blade, every bush and bird the centre of the surging. Far away somewhere is a church with a nose to sniff out heretics, a whip to chastise dreamers, and stones to kill prophets. Off in that other direction is a university; it has head trips and footnotes. Here above the river I sit among curiously familiar hummings and dronings and rustlings and goings. They appear; Eeyore asks why and Cindy shuts him up. You can't grasp the first cause, that's why because.

Spider comes hastening from somewhere,
over my canvas bag,
down the other side and away.

It's not what she was looking for.
That's why because.

OF BULLS AND BAPTISMS

I LOCK THE SUNBIRD WITH A CLICK OF THE KEY, check to see that I've parked far enough off the road, and turn toward the fence. Armed with a water bottle and a can of mosquito spray in a yellow plastic shopping bag, I part the barbed wire strands like this — there, I made it without ripping the back of my shirt or skewering my crotch — and walk into the heat along a scraggy downhill path in search of the old baptismal site, with swarms of mosquitoes coming toward me and as many grasshoppers jumping out of the way.

The remains of an old log barn sag there off to the right, walls slumped and half overgrown, roof long decomposed. I don't remember it there forty years ago, when I was fourteen at the time of my washing; but I recall people driving down in their cars, the community coming to see the latest batch of teenagers doused in the river. Once before I was baptized I was here with my cousin to go fishing. We made our way gingerly around a herd of cows overseen by a malevolent old bull, but we didn't catch any fish, and had to sneak back up again, cripes I hope there's no bull here now. I look around and estimate my chances, now at mid-life, of outrunning a bull and climbing a tree in front of a pair of tapered horns.

The path curves around a bluff, and I see the way is clear. Another shot of mosquito spray, another swallow of water, onward and down.

This need to be washed, to get clean. Starting over from scratch, opening your eyes for the first time on the first day in paradise, that's what the baptism was supposed to be about, death to the old and birth to the new. How could they have thought, how could *I* have thought, that a fourteen-year-old boy who had yet to travel more than a few miles from his village, who hadn't yet seen his first naked female body, had already become so jaded and soulsick, so hardbitten and worldly, that he needed to begin again?

The crazy thing is, I *was* sinsick. Maybe I hadn't seen a naked woman, but some of my older cousins had looked at men's magazines and told me about it, and the prospect of seeing them myself made me go weak with desire. Until bedtime, that is, when abruptly the Angel threatened again to appear as he had done to old Widow Giesbrecht in her shack on Railway Street. She claimed the Angel had healed her arm one night as she lay in bed after a pentecostal preacher laid hands on her in his tent on the sportsgrounds; look, she said, how I can move it up and down now where before it was all crippled up with rheumatism. But I was scared there would be no such goodwill toward me, that there'd be only an exposure of my reckless lust, and a command to atone for it by remaining celibate, or going away to Africa as a missionary like two of my uncles had done. I didn't want to see *that* angel.

Such were the defects and desperations that drove me down the aisles of the revival meetings and into the waters of baptism.

The path takes another turn and the ground levels off. I look back up the hill where no bull is yet to be seen, and the smell of prairie sage washes through me. It's not exactly beautiful, this landscape, but it has the starkness of home and the feel of many a boyish adventure. The prairie has its own kind of peace.

Well, get on with it, down to the river. An old rhythm-and-blues tune begins playing in my head: *Take me to the river, wash me in the water* . . .

That baptism at fourteen wasn't just a few drops of water on the head of a baby in a blanket, wrapped in the consoling arms of parents still silly with adoration. It was wading through mud into waist-deep water, kneeling so your chin just cleared the river, and being ducked under a swift current that threatened to carry you off and deposit you on a sandbar downriver somewhere near Fort Carlton. Yes we'll gather at the river, the people sang to us, where bright angels' feet have trod.

Here it is. A little field, and the rock where the deacons pitched the tents, one for the girls, one for the boys. I sit on the rock, take a draft of water, settle into the placid flow of the river.

Most summers when I was growing up, there came a Sunday when the church announced its intention to baptize. Those who felt ready — candidates, they were called — were advised to contact the minister. That fourteenth summer the announcement rolled off me again. I was a late bloomer a head shorter than my peers, and it had never occurred to me that I was old enough for this. But when I discovered that all the boys, including the cousin who fished here with me, had made their decision, I knew only that I didn't want to be left out and have to do it alone the next year, or with the younger candidates whose turn would come two summers later, and with much internal quaking I made up my mind to approach the Reverend.

I probably picked the worst possible time and place to do it. That summer the local evangelical churches had organized another of their week-long missionary conferences in the curling rink — which, like the winter revivals, regularly served to top up my guilt and fear — and at the end of one evening I pushed through the crowds in the aisle to get to the minister as he made his way to the exit. I can still see how far back I tilted my head to look into his face, a gentle face that smiled down as he patted my head in response to the blurt in which I made my wish known. I suppose he said it would be all right for me to be baptized, though I don't recall his words.

With this load off my mind, I hurried outside to my cousin's car, and was met with news he had just heard on the radio — Marilyn Monroe was dead. She had "checked off the roll," as he put it. What a waste, I thought sadly and with genuine shock, and wondered at his heartless way of announcing it.

But the relief of having spoken to the minister was short-lived, since the endorsement of baptismal candidates was a matter of such weight that his recommendation would need approval by the entire membership. My name was added to the list of those who would appear one night very soon before the congregation to be examined for suitability. There had been no formal classes; we were left to figure out as best we could what this affair was all about.

That evening as we drove the nine miles to our country church, I sat between my father and grandfather in the front seat of the Chevrolet Stylemaster — an old jalopy that so bitterly announced our poverty — while my mother and an aunt who lived with Grandpa sat in the back. As we turned onto the last stretch of gravel road, Grandpa felt led to instruct me. He had been rebaptized into the true faith when he married my grandmother — who was already buried in the cemetery ahead — and he pulled his German New Testament, translated by Martin Luther, from his black suitcoat and read me the account of Christ's baptism in the Jordan River.

"So if they ask you why you want to be baptized in a river," he concluded, "you tell them, 'Jesus was baptized in a river too.'"

That was it.

He had wanted to do me a service. What he had done was reconfirm his rejection of his own infant baptism in a little church in Zagorow, Poland in 1880; but that evening it did double duty as my catechism.

We parked in the churchyard, cemetery to our left, outdoor toilets to the right, empty old horse barns behind, and ahead of us the church which now I entered with foreboding.

The minister called the meeting to order. Promptly all candidates were charged to withdraw into the vestibules — girls into one and boys into the other — to await our summons. One by one we were recalled, to stand clutching our flappy black bibles before the somber faces in our unornamented church — men to our right, women to our left, any of whom had the privilege if not the duty of interrogating us. About anything they liked. For example, when and under what circumstances had we been saved? How thoroughly did we know the Bible? What did we plan to do about temptations to dance and smoke? For all we knew, someone might inquire openly about our sex lives, such as they were.

It was a hard night. I, for one, had broken down and cried before it was done, and it was one of my own relatives who drove me over the brim of my courage into the humiliation of public tears. He called on me to explain the meaning of baptism, and I believed I was ready with a text from St. Peter I had hunted up myself in the Authorized King James Version. It said something about baptism as "not the putting away of the filth of the flesh, but the answer of a good conscience toward God." I thought it was a pretty good text — not that I had a good conscience, but because it seemed to leave just a bit of room for a few private thoughts about Marilyn Monroe, and maybe a few more glimpses at *Life* magazine's pictures from her unfinished movie, where you knew she was naked hanging on the edge of that swimming pool and could only imagine what the photographer must have seen.

I read out my text, and after brief questioning, my uncle — himself an ordained minister, now home on summer vacation — saw that it would be necessary to illumine me. This he did emphatically and at great length, and concluded with his index finger jabbing the air toward me, "That Bible under your arm — read it!"

I went back along the aisle, wiping tears in front of the vestibule door, hoping the boys wouldn't notice, and sat on a bench under the coathooks to wait for the outcome of the vote, which was to be taken by a show of hands. At the end of the evening the minister announced that all the candidates, and I too, had been accepted, with what degree of reluctance or strength of majority we never knew. The minister himself had not questioned me; he only sat and observed, and a couple of Sunday afternoons later he baptized me.

Over there where the grass slopes down, the deacons had erected a handrail cut from green poplars to help us into the river. The onlookers gathered round while we candidates waited here by the tents. At the appointed hour a hymn was sung — Trust and obey For there's no other way To be happy in Jesus but to trust and obey — and we waded through the mud, steadied by the rails, and out into the current, I at the head of the line behind the minister. The black and white photos of this occasion show us taken in ascending order of size: how small I look there at the head of the line wearing another of my father's loathed haircuts, how much deeper the water is for me than for the others.

We baptized forwards, not backwards as certain other denominations did. The men of the church had debated the issue exhaustively, whether the death of Christ was more authentically pictured by the *forward* dunk, in token of his head's slumping forward on the cross when he gave up the ghost; or by the *backward* dunk, in token of his being laid on his back in the sepulchre. Forward was the right way, they had discerned. I wanted very much to think trusting and obedient thoughts as I entered the river, but I hadn't yet learned to swim and I feared suffocating under the muddy water; then as I knelt, and the bottom of the river shifted under my knees, I prayed that the current at my back wouldn't sweep me away — hadn't we heard so many warnings about the undertow and sharp drop-offs in that North Saskatchewan River?

Then it was over. I stumbled to the rear of the line and shook the water from my ears and watched the others going under. We waded back to shore and withdrew to the tents, the minister joining us in the boys' tent where we sat on the ground and got naked to dry ourselves and put on fresh clothes. I hastened into my shorts, trying to look pious yet nonchalant, and stole one shifty glance at the size of the Reverend's equipment — that minister who had baptized me, God bless him, without humiliating me further in my ignorance.

That night in church, in demonstration of our further obedience, we washed each other's feet in big enamel basins — another ordinance observed, like baptism, at the command of Christ. I washed my cousin's feet and he washed mine. Then we tore little chunks from a loaf of homemade bread and sipped Welch's grape juice from a goblet as these were passed from hand to hand along the pews; and afterwards we formed another lineup where the old members came to shake hands, finally, with the new ones. Welcome.

A mosquito stirs me back here to the rock. A pelican wheels overhead. Another shot of spray, another swallow of water.

What was it all about? Did they mean to scare the hell out of us? But if it had worked, I wouldn't be tempted to feel indignant. I had no idea what I was doing there in the river, any more than a blanketed baby at an ornate font. The baptism was to be done — I trusted and obeyed. In medieval times some waited till their deathbeds to request baptism, frightened of sinning after being washed and so damning themselves, scared to live after getting clean. Who ever knew what they were doing — infant, adolescent, or old-timer — when it was being done to them?

A few tears now, maybe a sort of baptism of desire, which some traditions also honoured like those of water, or fire, or spirit. If the doors of perception were cleansed, everything would appear infinite; I would be born again for the first time, have a fresh God walking and talking with my woman and me innocent in the evening in the garden. It happens sometimes, with or without baptism. When it happens, it is the baptism.

Back at the foot of the hill now. I sit for a moment on a log beside a grove of trees where some cattle are lying in the shade. If there's a bull among them, he's chewing his cud like the others, his tail busy with the mosquitoes.

Somewhere the crows are making a great commotion. And behind me, other little fowls of the air are tweedling in reply.

ARCHANGELS AND JINGLE BELLS

I Question not my Corporeal or Vegetative Eye any more than I would Question a Window concerning a Sight. I look thro' it & not with it.
— William Blake

𝒫ERCEPTIONS ARE ACTS OF CREATION. They can bring a dead world to life. They can replace the objective idols of our culture, and its disdain for our subjectivity, with images that point back at us when we see them. Lively images.

> *He thought he saw a Banker's Clerk*
> *Descending from the bus,*
> *He looked again, and found it was*
> *A hippopotamus.*

For more than a decade I worked as a therapist for children with emotional and behavioural difficulties. Sometimes we got into philosophical discussions which would go something like this.

"Is there such a thing as a real Santa Claus?" I'd ask.

"No there isn't," the sophisticated ones said, and went on to explain what really happens on Christmas Eve: "Your mom or dad just puts the presents under the tree after you go to sleep."

For others, skepticism had begun to intrude: "Some people say there is no Santa, but I think there is. But I don't know how he flies to all the houses in the world in one night, unless it's on a laser beam or something. Or maybe he brings the presents early and your parents hide them till Christmas."

"Well, is there such a thing as a real tooth fairy?" I'd ask.

Again the responses ranged from complete affirmative conviction ("Of course — she left money under my pillow.") to bold denial, even scorn ("My mom puts the money there and pretends it's the tooth fairy").

So I would proceed through the range of mythical and fairy tale beings — trolls to witches to easter rabbits — until I got to the angels. Angels die hard for children, and if there's been even a dribble of religious sentiment in their homes, angels are there, somehow, long after the other characters have been debunked.

"How do you know there are real angels?" I'd ask. And they'd reply, "Because when you die, the angels come and take you up to heaven."

That's how we know these things.

Alas for the angels, they are almost certain to go the way of gnomes and unicorns, or of the ghosts my daughter saw coming from a car's tailpipe one winter day. When William Blake was a child he saw a tree full of angels, and he kept seeing them throughout his life — in the sunrise, hovering over the heads of men harvesting grain. But for most of us, as the prophet knew, our hearts have waxed gross and our eyes are shut.

One year at Advent, the jingle bells were long out of their boxes and I had again resisted shopping until this was no longer feasible. I spent an evening flying around the city and among the malls, craving a silent night where shepherds huddle beneath blinking stars, and magicians push westward on slow camels toward a manger where cattle are lowing as a baby awakes. Finally I went to relax in front of the fireplace with Larraine, whom I would soon marry, and well after midnight I took a leisurely way home. I followed Spadina Crescent along the river from the north end of the city, skirted downtown, crossed the Victoria Avenue steel bridge, and drove beside the river again to my apartment at the south end of town, next to Diefenbaker Park. No jingle-jangle anywhere in that ancient plod toward the stable.

I pulled into the parking lot and got out, and stretched in the night air. By tradition one is inclined to look for angels in the sky; sometimes they hang there over the balcony of heaven and tell those who are sore afraid to relax. But I wasn't thinking about angels; I was cherishing the silence, feeling grateful that it was still possible, occasionally, to be in the city and not hear any noise.

I looked up to see the stars, and there was an Archangel. I could tell by the size. It hovered directly over the parking lot, one huge pinion spread out over the river toward the AgPro grain terminal on the western horizon, the other stretching east toward the Circle Drive Alliance Church — as if to say, Peace, if not on earth, then on this part of Saskatoon, of which the Sundowner Apartment parking lot is the centre. The wingspan of an ordinary angel measures about twelve feet from tip to tip, I think Aquinas had determined somewhere in the *Summa Theologiae*; but this one must have measured four or five miles across, so it was an archangel, brooding over the bent world with warm breast and with ah! bright wings.

A moment later I saw northern lights — and I fought with my gross-waxing heart until a song began playing, *Schafe koennen sicher weiden*, sheep may safely graze . . . Oh no, said William Blake, don't suppose I see something round and gold in the sky that looks somewhat like a guinea; I see angels and I hear them sing. So I don't say I looked up from the parking lot and saw an aurora borealis. For one instant I saw the archangel Gabriel on shimmering wings above Ste. Cecilia Avenue, offering peace to someone who intends, if not always achieves, genuine goodwill toward the world.

When I sat down to write this, I was curious to know the meaning of aurora borealis. Aurora, I find, is the Roman goddess of dawn, and borealis is something that pertains to the north. So it could have been the goddess of the northern night. But I call it an archangel.

And I know that if a parishioner from the Alliance Church had stood in his parking lot that night, he would have been right underneath Gabriel too.

Because the centre of the world is everywhere.

NO BISCUIT BLUES

*O*NE SUNDAY AFTERNOON WHEN I WAS TEN or twelve years old, in an upstairs bedroom of my uncle's farmhouse I found a blood-red booklet titled *The Lake of Fire*, which nearly impaired forever my capacity to trust. The cover showed contorted bodies leaping and falling back into a lake of molten sulphurous bubbles, and a man at the head of a long line flailing at hell's brink with eyes bulging and fists grabbing the air. The text told how the doomed would try to escape, how they would be driven down nevertheless by the order of the Judge: "Away!" I tried to fathom this Jekyll-and-Hyde Christ, who was said to be compassionate and forgiving though we have sinned against Him, yet who would come with a sword in His mouth to smite the nations and tread the winepress of the fierce wrath of Almighty God.

About that time I also received a monthly magazine from a well-known evangelical organization. One especially vivid issue showed a great stone pyramid with a legion of steps mounting to a platform at its top, where Jesus or God sat on a resplendent and awful throne. On judgment day, the writer said, I would be summoned from an ocean of people to mount those steps, to hear my life reviewed in the presence of celestial, terrestrial, and infernal powers — and what chance would I have there, shrivelled up before Omnipotence unleashed? Like the Rev. Sprague in *Tom Sawyer*, my tradition "dealt in limitless fire and brimstone and thinned the predestined elect down to a company so small as to be hardly worth the saving."

Most of my peers also claimed to take this religion seriously. They went forward in the revival crusades, testified in church and around campfires, toted bibles to Sunday school, and were baptized at the age of fourteen-to-sixteen. But what they didn't seem to do was suffer. They cracked jokes about the Holy Ghost with never a worry over the unpardonable sin, they groped their girls, they tooled around on motorcycles while I looked on enviously. Believe in the Lord Jesus Christ or be damned — this was the first and greatest commandment of my childhood church, that curious hybrid between sixteenth-century Anabaptism and nineteenth-century frontier revivalism; and I believed every word they told me, even if others only pretended to believe, or thought they believed.

It was a philosophical disaster, of course, with its heaven and hell sitting side by side forever, each attesting to the other's failure. I didn't outgrow it as swiftly as I wished, or as some others seemed to do. After high school I went to a fundamentalist institution which many of my relatives had attended, found a wife there, became the father of two daughters, spent seven years as a minister in my own denomination, and lost thirty pounds of weight. Then, it seemed, I was ready.

At the age of thirty-one I enrolled in graduate studies in psychology at the University of Saskatchewan, where I had been awarded a scholarship. My family and I began attending a large United Church, where shortly — and to me incredibly — I was hired as an assistant to the minister. This launched a heady period of life, where for the first time I was out from under fundamentalism's surveillance. I felt more powerful than ever before, and finally began doing what one of my professors said most others do at the age of fourteen.

It was intoxicating. The easy dismissal of old strictures. The enthusiastic reception by wealthy professionals of the largest and most liberal Protestant denomination in Canada — people cried when I gave my first sermon there, I who had sprung from a Mennonite company of fewer than twenty churches worldwide. The ease with which graduate studies came, where the educated agnostic community embraced me as ardently as my new-found religious world did. It was a quantum leap after clogged decades. "My little finger is thicker than my father's loins," I thought.

It was hardly fair, a village boy thrown into the largesse I was shown then, and I grew inordinately bold. I found my tradition pathetic, and began having great fun lampooning it. In the vein of Ambrose Bierce, I created my own *Devil's Dictionary*. I defined "atonement" as a doctrine affirming that God had once displaced his wrath onto a human scapegoat, in order that we might learn to forgive each other freely. "Communion" I defined as eating plastic tiddly-winks and drinking grape juice after having flagellated oneself into a proper sense of worthlessness. A "disciple" seemed to me a parrot, an ape, a copycat. "Evangelism" was the proclamation of bad news, designed to throw the good news into relief; and "literal" was a style of biblical interpretation in which literary considerations were forfeit. And so on.

This playing with fire lasted for months. One day the senior pastor returned in irritation from the United Church's national conference. He said they'd spent more time debating a resolution to levy surcharges against corporations using more than x-kilowatt hours of electricity per month, than they had on matters concerning the human soul and spirit, and he was starting to wonder whether this was really what a church is for. I was reading Alan Watts at the time, who predicted that any religion failing to return to its origins in mystical experience will eventually become another mindless fundamentalism or another political redundancy. It seemed to me he was right.

It didn't take long for me also to be disillusioned with North American psychology. Gordon Allport had accused it of preoccupation with rats, machines, and infants, and so incapable of advancing to the central and symbolic issues of human life. I thought he was right, too.

My time with the United Church ended after graduate studies, when I was offered a temporary position as a counsellor in a Roman Catholic school division. This seemed an ideal opportunity to earn the first proper salary of my life, while at the same time looking around for what to do next, and soon I had settled into my first Catholic high school. A day came when mass was to be celebrated, and I asked the chaplain, Father Beechinor, whether I might attend and receive communion. He assured me I was welcome at mass; communion, he said with an apologetic chuckle, was for Catholics.

Catholic worship was fascinating and colourful and profound, centred on ritual at an altar rather than the outworn fulminations from a pulpit. I loved the ceremony and the liturgy, I loved the unsparing welcome I was given in every other respect. But after a time I saw those colleagues and students lined up again and again, so hopefully or so routinely, counting on the priest to make the Real Presence present, and finally the point of communion became for me the point of separation. I craved to be included.

But one thing leads to another. I was offered a permanent contract, and accepted it gladly. Many asked how a former Protestant minister came to be a counsellor in a Catholic school system. I replied that I didn't know, though I certainly had been made welcome. Still, I often imagined one day I might return to the ministry — hoping, I suppose, for another chance to unravel my Christianity's graveclothes — and after three years, when an invitation came from a more tolerant wing of my tradition, I left education and became a pastor again. There, after only fourteen months, marriage and ministry came to a simultaneous end, my wife having become adamant about reclaiming our fundamentalist heritage, and I more determined than ever to be rid of it. My presence quickly disappointed some of the very parishioners who so lately had applauded my ignition of new heat in a church gone cold, and one day when the separations had begun to loom, I visited Father Beechinor, who by now had become a good friend, and who welcomed me as warmly as ever.

"Others can call me Father," he said, "you call me Ron, please."

He listened to my story and said without hesitation, "If you separate, you're welcome to come and work here again. If you divorce, you're welcome to come back. And you don't want to think about this now, but if you ever remarry, you're welcome to work with us here."

Then almost as an afterthought he added, "If you were Catholic, I wouldn't be able to say it to you quite this way." He meant that his church allowed him to be more charitable to me than it did to members of his own flock. But what he had actually done, perhaps without realizing it, was to give me the sacrament after all. His compassion was the one form of grace I still found meaningful, for it incarnated a trust such as my heritage wouldn't — or couldn't — give, since its grace was more a theological contrivance than a living experience. I went back to the Catholic schools and stayed for another eleven years.

Now began a time of finding grace greater than all my sins, as the words of a childhood hymn went. It came in the most surprising ways, and with just the incongruity to which Father Beechinor had referred: you can't expect as freehanded a blessing from your own religious home as you can find elsewhere. I basked in Catholicism's generosity toward me, while some of my colleagues chafed under its imperiousnesss toward them.

But it was by no means only through Catholicism that graces came. They came also through eastern traditions and joyful pagans; through books and music; through animals in the park, dreams in the bedroom, children who loved me; and finally through Larraine, who after long patience with my fear and vacillation became my partner. One day I read where Erich Fromm said that God's name — I Am What I Am — means, approximately, My name is Nameless. I lost interest in debates about whether God is a mist or a mist-maker; I no longer knew what I meant by the word, only why I wanted to use it sometimes, and other times not. Owen Barfield says most nouns are the names of idols, and the noun God is no exception. The Lakota, on the other hand, use a term which is pure adjective: Great Mysterious.

By the time I had spent a dozen years in little rooms with troubled people, the life of writing which had called me since adolescence was beginning to knock urgently. At the end of fourteen years, and naturally with mixed emotions, I resigned.

In the last Catholic school where I worked, I had become friends with Rick Lesko, the lay chaplain. All the students there were designated "alternate", meaning they came riddled with scurvy histories and twisted emotions, with academic defeats and endless skirmishes with the law. They were contemporary lepers, and we who worked with them often doubted the adequacy of our help.

One night near the end of that last year, I woke from a dream which reinforced again my long habit of turning the sensors inward at the threshold of sleep. I had been saying Good Friday mass in a Catholic church. The homily was done, the liturgy was far advanced, and the time for communion had come. The crowd began forming a line, but not in front of me. It was, of course, to the priest they went — that same priest who had deprived me of the host so long ago only to give it to me privately in another form.

Still, I was dejected. There were my friends again waiting their turn to consume Christ, most of whom stood, like I, in perpetual need of grace. Why should I who had worked and prayed and transgressed with them be excluded again? I turned to Lesko and told him my sadness.

He went at once to Father Beechinor and whispered something in his ear. He came trotting back with a clenched right fist, halted in front of me and began reciting the Lord's Prayer at top speed, stuffing my mouth with the chocolate he had concealed in his hand. By the time he got to "deliver us from evil" my cheeks were bulging like Dizzy Gillespie blowing his trumpet; for an instant Lesko and I stared big-eyed at each other, then we doubled over in laughter. Off to the side were children in chairs tilting down and up in a game they called Resurrection, like weeble-wobbles knocked down and forever springing up again. A line of adults devoutly swallowed wafers, a bunch of kids played resurrection, and I woke up in very good spirits indeed. Later over coffee I told Lesko the dream and made him laugh too.

Soon afterward the final mass of the year was celebrated. The ordinarily dull gymnasium had been decorated with our students' creations; the good Father had vested himself again; a choir of thin voices launched bravely into the bars of an entrance hymn, and the mass got under way.

I sat far to the back. This was another of the routines concluding the academic year; for me it was also the last rites of an institutional career. My gratitude toward these friends was intact, but I was ready for a writing adventure. I mumbled along with the liturgy; at the designated places I crossed myself; I listened to my priest straining to tell our outcaste students that they too were loved and lovable. I knew there would be no wafer for me. I had a touch of the No Biscuit Blues — but never mind, said I, this is the last time, from now on there will be plenty of wafers in the world glad to give themselves.

When the time came for the sign of peace, I rose with the crowd. I shook the Catholic hand of a man ten years divorced, who only last night had given and received a certain ecstasy with the woman his church hadn't yet recognized as one of its own. I shook another hand, and from the corner of my eye saw the lay chaplain hastening around the back of the gym, shaking hands along the way — then he was before me saying *The peace of Christ be with you*, pressing something into my hand and gone again with his wind bringing peace to others. I looked down and there was a half-melted chocolate bar in my fist, of the kind a current TV commercial was calling sinfully indulgent. I hustled it out of sight and shook my head, and tried to bottle the mirth rising in my gut.

When the candles were snuffed out, and the altar was silent and the gym gone dark, when the priest and the secretaries and teachers were drinking coffee in their lounge, I stole into the first private spot I could find. And there in the company of a potter's kiln and a dozen ceramic Jesuses on a shelf, I consumed the sacrament under the species of chocolate, and shared the last laugh.

Grace makes me laugh.

SWEAT

*T*HE FIRST TIME I INVOKED THE GRANDFATHERS was the day my first grandson was born. The message came from Winnipeg just before I left for a bush a few hours north of Saskatoon, where an initiate of the Bear clan had offered to help me through my first ceremonial sweat in his lodge. Ramsy said Tommy was fine, my daughter Shannon was fine; it was a bright and melodious spring day, and it seemed to me everybody should have such a drive to the bush as I had.

Others had been invited, but when the time came, only the Bear and I were on hand. He invited me to join in the preparations, and explained the clan's traditional ways as we went. Together we built the fire, together we transported stones, in concert we circled the lodge — he outside, I from the inside — to seal it against the light. I fretted at my clumsiness, but this was of no concern to the Bear. Nor did it matter that I had no aboriginal blood in me, or that he was the director of an institute where I worked, and so, in the strict sense, was my chief. He cared only that we sweat together in the old way, take an aboriginal remedy for the ancient ill: *You shall give birth to your children in pain; with sweat on your brow shall you eat bread till you return to the soil* — the joy of Tommy's life, and ours, attended by the pain.

When the stones were hot, we carried them inside. At the door, the Bear performed the pipe ritual; then he handed the pipe to me and helped me repeat the words again. I turned its stem to the six directions, invoked the Grandfathers, offered a pinch of my favourite tobacco. Then we crawled in.

As with a penitent in a confessional, or a soul pouring out a heartful to a therapist, nothing said in a sweat lodge is to be repeated elsewhere. It is not forbidden, however, to try to describe the sweat.

The Bear dipped a pine branch into water and shook it toward the stones, which hissed to life and commenced an exorcism. Amid the clan's old laughing songs and crying songs, we wet the branch by turns and spattered the stones — radiant stones — and there was a short, futile struggle with claustrophobia, then surrender, and beyond that the noises of my laughter and tears mingling with the Bear's. If sweat belongs to Adam's curse, it pertains also to the cure. Nowhere to run, nowhere to hide. And I laughed and cried for Tommy, for the orbit to which he was rising and the bittersweetness of the coming circles; laughed and cried for both of us, all of us, in one shaking with two meanings, or a life of meanings.

We came outside for a moment, breathed blessed air and drank water, and crawled in and did it again, the stones from the centre seeking out intentions deeper than our lives' broken promises. And after three rounds of this — perhaps an hour of clock time — it was over.

We sat outside in our chairs, body and mind together, in a clearing in a bush where infinite calm was. We waited not in expectation, but in fulfillment. It was a patriarchal moment, to be sure — archetypal Grandfathers, grandpa and grandson, two men in a furnace — yet the grandness was greater than the maleness. I had repented of white man's time, and it was good.

The next morning, Mother's Day, I woke up ravenously hungry. I had blistered the tip of my nose. So furiously had I splattered the stones, and generated such intense heat, that unawares I had forged for myself an emblem of the ordeal, just faintly like the patriarch Jacob's basted hip after his contention with the dark spirit.

Soon I had places to go, people to see, things to do — my grilled nose ahead of me running from Indian time, straight into the accumulation of fresh dross for the old fire.

The Bear says I'm welcome back any time. Purgatory beckons.

THE BARRIER OF THE PATRIARCHS

A FRIEND DROVE INTO THE COUNTRY ONE DAY to inspect a test plot for the Canada Research Council. On many previous trips he had passed a turkey farm, and for once his curiosity got the better of him. Hundreds of cages stood there, each containing a bird; but one door hung from a broken hinge, and a turkey stood on the threshold, diminutive head peering into the world, body bulking safe in the cage till Thanksgiving. Darryl called it a Far Side cartoon.

The Zen master Mumon once gave the following talk to his students. You must pass through the barrier of the patriarchs, he said. To do this, you will have to work through every bone in your body and every pore in your skin. It will feel as if you have a hot iron ball stuck in your throat — you can't swallow it and you can't spit it out. Then your previous ideas will disappear; your subjectivity and your objectivity will become one. You will be crushed to death, but you will shake the heaven and move the earth. You will become like a great warrior with a sharp sword: if a Buddha stands in your way, you cut him down, if a patriarch blocks you, you kill him. Then any world you enter, you enter as if it were your playground.

The mystics of all traditions know that "theists" tend to believe their metaphors are facts, while "atheists" know their metaphors are not facts, and are therefore lies. Mystics may use traditional language, but they are speaking mythologically; their symbols concern spiritual events, and historicity — or its lack — is incidental to their truth. Patriarchs, on the other hand, want us to use words literally, as they themselves use them. St. John of the Cross wrote poetry and theological tomes with the Spanish Inquisition breathing down his neck, and even so was accused of being a disguised Buddhist; his religion was like a sponge, one superior said — still intact when all the Christianity had been wrung out of it.

Richard Russo tells of being raised Roman Catholic and remaining a devout adherent until the age of ten, when suddenly he became afflicted with psychosomatic fits of suffocating, vomiting, and swooning every time he went to church, until his exasperated parents finally stopped making him go. By college age he considered himself an agnostic with his Catholicism far behind him. Then as he approached thirty, he was visited by a series of what he called "Catholic dreams".

In one of them, he was involved in a plot to assassinate the Pope. He carried a package of poison to the top of a cathedral tower, from where he was to drop it on signal when the Pope entered. But as cardinals and bishops began processing, he dropped the poison too soon, and racing downstairs to retrieve it, he found himself unaccountably kneeling at the altar rail as the Pope was saying high mass. Behind the altar stood a life-sized crucifix with a living figure on it. And when the Pope said, "We are all in the service of Christ," the figure from the cross blessed the people, turned to Russo and smiled, and said, "Even you, Russo." That was the end of his interest in assassination plots.

A master was once asked who the Buddha was, and replied, "The cat climbs the post." The disciple confessed his inability to grasp the meaning, and the master said, "If you don't understand, ask the post." D. T. Suzuki comments on this: "The cat is not enveloped with a halo; the post has no resemblance to the Cross. When Christians stand all naked, shorn of their dualistic garments, they will discover that their God is no other than the Absolute Present itself."

Why must the patriarchal barrier be broken through? So that we are not diverted by dogmas of a Christ growing in wheat but not in rice. So that women are not cowed by decrees, canons, ordinances, and regulations about how high they shall be allowed to ascend. So that patriarchs stop raping us and leaving us with "the emotions that persist after the facts have faded," as a graduate student said in a discussion of childhood sexual abuse. So that the religion *of* Jesus doesn't turn into doggerel *about* Jesus, where dead scriptures are more important than living persons, and where past and future are pirates of the eternal Now.

Sometimes when the Pope celebrates mass, a dead idol behind him comes to life and says "Even you." I can't hear it saying like an archbishop, "A rice-wafer in church is both illegal and ineffective," just as I can't imagine Mumon, or Russo, literally killing literal patriarchs.

Why must we pass through the barrier? So we're not turkeys in broken cages. So any world we enter becomes our playground. Even a world of patriarchs.

O WHEEL

*T*HE MAYOR OF DACHAU TAKES FOR GRANTED we are not here to see the town. "Dear Guests," the brochure begins, "You have come to Dachau to visit the memorial site in the former Concentration Camp. Innumerable crimes were committed. Like you, the citizens of Dachau bow their heads before the victims of this camp. After your visit, you will be horror-stricken. But we sincerely hope you will not transfer your indignation to the ancient 1200-year-old Bavarian town of Dachau, which was not consulted when the concentration camp was built and whose citizens voted quite decisively against the rise of National Socialism . . . "

There are photos, then, of footpaths beside the Muehlbach River, and distant Alps as seen from the Dachau Palace. There are paintings of old mills and taverns and smithies, and of harvests and peat bogs, of the place as it was before the years of infamy.

"I extend a cordial invitation to you to visit the old town of Dachau," the mayor says. "We would be pleased to greet you within our walls and to welcome you as friends."

Today in the death camp schoolchildren climb on the wrought-iron gate, hanging around its *ARBEIT MACHT FREI* while their teachers snap pictures. The *Wirtschaftsgebauede* is a museum now, where a movie replays images of gaunt Jews looking out through that same gate; where a painting titled "The Public Enemy" shows the patched back of a shrivelled man with his nose to a brick wall, about to be shot — the painter, A. Paul Weber, himself having been imprisoned by the Nazis for his resistance. A kiosk at the door offers to sell us a picture book of remembrances.

Just outside the wall, where the trains unloaded their human cattle, Carmelite nuns have built a convent, and inside are Christian chapels, each denomination with its own. The Jewish memorial is shaped like an oven above ground; black-barbed rails border a ramp leading down to a padlocked gate, through which we peer and see nearly nothing inside — a book, a flower, a single shaft of light from a hole in the ground above.

We stand in the gas chamber and look. We put our heads into the ovens and look.

Near the exit, a monument says *Never Again*. We don't speak as we leave the camp — we cry, or we are sick in our stomachs.

Our guidebook urges us not to miss the Kloster Andechs a few kilometres south of Dachau, where monks brew Klosterhof beer and serve oversize helpings of German food. We drive uphill through a forest, tuck our rented Opel between tour buses, and climb still higher to the patios adjoining a pink tenth-century church — four or five of them — where beer gardens are in full career. The *Bierstube* is the most stupendous mess hall we've ever seen, and we stand in line for the ham, sauerkraut, and potato salad specialty. A ruddy monk asks, *Fuer eins oder zwei?* I hold up two fingers and he points at a ham hock with jagged bones protruding. I nod, expecting him to slice, but he seizes it by the bone and passes it to his brothers, who plop sauerkraut and salad on plates — enough for two strong men and a boy — and the line flows back out to the patios where tourists sit under open tents, and wrinkled seniors from the buses wander about merrily with steins of beer almost too big to hold in one hand.

So the wheels of existence run: stout monks brewing Klosterhof and chanting vespers here, scapegoats mangled and burned there — see how their smoke rises and forms into clouds, and drifts away. *Work Frees* — is that so? "As for the wheels," Ezekiel said, "it was cried unto them in my hearing: O wheel." We walk from the church with a bellyful of beer and sauerkraut, and the wheel turns.

In a funeral chapel at home Jim's three-year-old granddaughter asks, "What's Grandpa doing in that manger?" The next day under a lowering firmament, in a wind that nearly knocks us over, we bury him where his fourteen-year-old daughter lies in the prairie; and as we adults weep, Karlee plays so happily around the grave that we fear she'll fall in. We leave Jim in the earth and wheel away, yearning toward the child's unwillingness to interpret, her willing immersion in the next thing, and the next. O wheel.

A casket, a manger. What is that ray of light doing in the oven?

WILLY BECKER AND THE SOUTH CHURCH

THE NAME OF LITTLE WILLY BECKER'S VILLAGE, Adair, Saskatchewan, may seem kind of funny at first when you think how many Mennonites live here. You would have expected, maybe, something like Blumenheim or Schnetjedarp. But those villages are all quite far away, twenty or thirty miles, places Willy has only heard about here in Adair where he lives.

You are probably wondering why is the village called Adair, and not one of those other names that, as I say, maybe you expected? Well, Pete Hamm he explained it to me once, the Pete Hamm that works in the Village Office and goes to the North Church. He said Adair was the back name of a certain politician who was quite famous at one time when this part of the country was still the Northwest Territories. Pete couldn't remember the front name, but this Mr. Adair had done some quite important things. It's just escaped me now what they were, or maybe Pete never got around to telling me, but as I say, they were such important things that Adair got a village named after him, and this is that village, with more than three hundred people, where Willy Becker has lived all his eleven years.

You can't call it exactly a Mennonite village. There are three Catholic families here, if you count the Sudermans who farm along the road to the Number Eleven. But they have to go fifteen miles to Emery Lake when they want to go to church, which I've heard tell they do sometimes. And there are more Lutherans even than Catholics: around twenty families, counting the farmers from the Pine Point area two miles northwest. They have their own church with a bell-tower close by the Beckers' house, that was moved in from Pine Point around 1950 when Willy was a kid. So you can't say exactly that Adair is a Mennonite village, but still there are enough Mennonites here that they haven't all been able to fit into one church, so there is the North Church that Pete Hamm goes to and the South Church where the Beckers go, with maybe thirty or forty families each. One stands a block north of Main Street, and the other a block south, so they're exactly the same distance from the big intersection with the Imperial Bank on one side and Art's Store on the other, and pretty near half the village is in between them.

Sooner or later I'm going to tell you about the time when Willy Becker came to such a state in his life that he knew it was time to get saved. If you are not too sure what that means, don't worry, it will all get cleared up as we go along. I'll only say that it had something to do with going into Peggy Hinz's bedroom one Sunday night after Christian Endeavor in the South Church, where the Beckers and Hinzes both belong, and letting her talk him into taking down his pants in exchange for her raising up her dress. Although that sin never came out into the light of day, not so far anyway, and after awhile Willy could even forget about it sometimes, still it was the start of something that led to something else — you know how it is — and in the long run it ended up by him stealing a pack of Vogue cigarettes from Art's store. He never smoked them, mind you, because while he was getting brave enough to steal them, he never thought about planning how to smoke them, and those Vogues landed up in a poplar bush by the village well where Adairites pump their drinking water. For sure Willy had committed more sins than these, but it was when he stole the Vogues that for some reason he really became scared, considering his knowledge about hell and everything, that as I mentioned, he finally decided it was time to get saved.

But you should maybe know a little more about the South Church, and some of the differences with the North Church, if you're going to understand me right about Little Willy's conversion. Some of the differences are quite complicated, as you will see, while others are more or less out in the open, so much so that if the Beckers had happened to belong to the North Church, Willy wouldn't have actually needed to get saved at all. But as I say, this will get clearer as we go along.

I already pointed out how the two churches stand in opposite directions from Main Street, which runs east and west, which is why they are called the North and South Church. You'd notice a lot of other differences pretty soon if you lived here in Adair. For instance, the North Church is attended by both P. K. Friesen and P. P. Friesen, while in the South Church there is only a P. L. Friesen. Similarly, Little Jake Martens goes to the South Church, but Big Jake, who is related to him pretty close (he is cousin-uncle over Little Jake's mother-in-law) goes to the North. There's only one Elmer in Adair, Elmer Unger, who goes sometimes to the North Church, but not his English wife; and only one Rudolph, which is Rudy Regier who goes to the South. But both churches have Corneys — Corney Willems and Corney Dirks in the South, Corney Epp and Corney Friesen in the North. And there are ministers named Pete in both cases. Rev. Pete Nickel preaches in the South Church, and Rev. Pete Thiessen in the North. The South Church has about five Willems families, but in the North Church you won't find a single Willems of any kind. In the same way, Jake P. Dyck, who farms a mile out of town, goes to the North Church and smokes right out in the open; while Jake D. Dyck attends the South and only smokes in the granary behind his caragana hedge two miles from town.

For another thing, the North Church is made up of half farmers and half village people, while in the South Church it's the other way around. In the South the young boys sit by themselves in the front benches, whereas in the North the boys of that age sit up in the balcony. They have green hymnbooks in the North Church called *Songs of Faith and Life*, and in the South there are blue books called *Choice Hymns of the Faith*. And so on.

Anybody can see these things easily if they happen to go first into one church and then into the other. But some of the differences are a little harder to understand. For example, in the North Church they have a big motto on the wall behind the pulpit that says "Let all generations praise the Lord", whereas in the South Church a motto of roughly the same size and hanging at the same place says "Prepare to meet thy God". Again, in the South Church the collection bags are made out of dark blue velvet and passed from hand to hand between the people in the benches. In the North Church they have exactly such velvet bags but they are attached to long wooden poles, so the ushers can reach them in and out of the benches from where they stand in the aisle, so in the North Church it's not really necessary for most of the people to handle the money bags at all.

That reminds me: in both churches the men sit on the left side facing the motto at the front — the Praise or Prepare motto, as the case may be — and the women sit on the right (although from the viewpoint of the ministers it's the other way around). The young boys, as I say, will sit either in the front benches away from their parents, or up in the balcony by themselves, according to whichever church they go — in that way they are the same. The families are separated in an orderly way in both churches, but in one case they face north and in the other west, because of how the churches are built on their lots. So you see what I mean.

Then there are the annual meetings, where you have quite a noticeable difference. In the North Church they are called brotherhood meetings, only the members never actually say to each other "Brother Quiring" or "Brother Penner"; whereas in the South Church they are called business sessions, but they address each other as "Brother So-and-so", let's say when they're discussing a question like whether the piano needs to be tuned this year.

"I don't agree with Brother Willems," Transport Klassen might say, "I think we have enough musical talent right here in our midst that we could borrow a tuning fork and do it ourselves."

And then Brother Corny Willems might take the floor and say, "Brother Klassen is right that we have lots of talent, but I heard that Frank Janzen from Hofnungsfeld doesn't charge all that much," and so on.

Here is another difference between the churches — or maybe it's something they have the same, if you want to look at it that way. In the North Church there are quite a few brothers named Epp or Bergen or Peters, but none named Labossiere or Xiaopeng. While in the South there are Klassens and Reimers and Rempels, but no Bigskys or Kermeens. In the North you have a brother called Hamm but none called Hammond, and again in the South you have lots of members named Peters but no Peterson. So I think you see my point.

In both the North and South Church there are some people that are never called by their right names. Transport Klassen in the South, for example, is called that way because he drives a transport back and forth to Saskatoon every day, hauling steers and pigs to Intercontinental Packers, and bananas or rice krispies back again to Art's Groceteria and the Adair Co-op, which he's done for so many years that only the old folks know his real name. In the same way, the North Church has a brother called Egg Enns who runs the candling station, and nobody from Willy's generation knows his right name either. In the South there is a Mr. Fast who is a few bales short of a load, so they call him Slow Fast but not right to his face; and in the North there is a Pracha Peters who they say is quite poor, who often goes visiting with an empty shopping bag and comes back home with something in it. By the way, there's also a Barn Schmidt in Adair who doesn't go to any church except when there is a funeral. He's not a farmer; he's called that way because of his breath.

When it comes to baptism, there are several differences in the two churches. Whereas in the North they pour water on the people right inside their church, if the South wants to have a baptism they wait till summer and go to the river on a Sunday afternoon and duck their people underwater. Sprinklers in the North and dippers in the South, you could say. And you should listen once to some South Church brothers — they spend a lot more time discussing the differences than North Churchers do, I'll tell you that. Like you'd maybe hear Willy's uncle Harry Becker standing outside the Chinese Cafe with Little Jake Martens talking about baptism. Meanwhile Central Sawatzky from the North Church would be out in the country on top of a telephone pole with a long cigarette holder in his teeth; he wouldn't even be thinking about baptism, he'd be replacing an insulator that somebody had shot out and thinking, "I bet it's that *vedollt* P. L. Friesen's kid from the South Church that did this again." And Uncle Harry would tell Little Jake, "I heard they baptized Central's boy last Sunday in the North Church. How can those people do that? You should of seen him tearing around with Central's car behind the Community Hall last week."

"Well, that's how they are," Little Jake would say, "their kids repeat the catechism and then they think they're saved. And after catechism class I bet they go for a smoke behind their church. My son Abe he always wants to hang around with those North Church guys. It's a good thing the revival meetings are coming again, not so?"

Maybe now you can see how the order is a little different in the two churches. In the South, first you are reminded about your sins until you feel quite bad about it, then you get saved, and a couple of summers later they duck you in the river and make you a member. Whereas in the North it's like this: first you say the catechism, then you maybe go and have a smoke, and in a few Sundays they pour water on your head and you're automatically a brother, like that. This difference may not seem too important to you, but as I say, here in Adair it reaches quite a ways, even up to the insulators on the telephone poles.

Lately it's been reaching pretty hard into Little Willy Becker's head too. He sees clear enough that North Church kids never think about getting saved or lost — that's more or less what you'd expect from people who think it's so easy to get into heaven. And the Catholics, they don't even count — Billy McRae smokes right in front of his parents, and not filter tips either. But it bothers Willy that even some South Church kids don't worry about it. Little Jake's right about Abe — he smokes all the time in the stockyard barn. And Neil Dirks says he is saved, but then he shows Royce Peters that plastic viewer with the naked woman that he hides in his hayloft. Or you take like Willy's cousin Tim — he is saved already too, but he brags how he accidentally bumps into Gracie Neufeld's tits all the time, and how can somebody with their head full of such not be scared about hell and God? Not that Willy wouldn't like to see that viewer — but Neil has never offered to show him, and in a way it's good, because if he did Willy would look. And all those bake sales the North Church has every year to raise money for the MCC, they don't do much to make people think about their sins, whereas in Willy's church there are revivals and crusades, and anybody can see how there's a difference between a bake sale and getting saved, and if only the Beckers went to the North Church,

Willy would be looking at the motto that says Praise instead of the one that says Prepare.

So Willy's scared about the upcoming revival all right, what the preacher from the States will say — he remembers it clear enough from last year. But then he hadn't piled up such important sins, and it wasn't so hard to stay sitting in the bench when they sang Just As I Am Without One Plea.

Still, in a kind of weird way he's almost glad the meetings are coming. Maybe he'll have to finally clear all that up about Peggy and the Vogues and other things.

Then, Willy figures, maybe God will leave him alone for awhile.

A MEDICINE STORY

*N*EAR THE END OF THE SECOND GRADE, I got into my first fight on the school playground with a younger but bigger and heavier kid nicknamed Big Ears. We had shoved at each other awhile when he stuck out his foot and tripped me, and I went for a hard tumble. I tried to break the fall, and did — but also broke the bones of my right arm about six inches above the wrist.

It was 1954. Before the days of medicare nobody in our world was in a hurry to see a doctor, and it was a long time before anyone knew those bones were broken. Our remedies began close to home. Across the back alley lived an old woman who had a reputation as a "bone-setter". These were homegrown practitioners who applied coarse remedies to assorted ailments, including broken bones. My people preferred consulting them over doctors because their fees were negotiable, ranging from a heartfelt *Dankeschoen* to maybe a bag of potatoes from the garden, or even an occasional cash payment of a dollar or two. In the Low German dialect, they were known as *Traijtmoakasch* — rightmakers. My paternal grandfather was a well-known rightmaker in the district, operating a clinic from a little yellow shed in his backyard under a sign that read "Dew

Drop Inn". He had strong liniments there, and many sizes of wooden crutches on which we cousins hobbled around his yard when we went for family gatherings. But the clinic was eight miles away in the next village, while old Mrs. Sawatzky lived next door.

My mother and I sat down at her kitchen table. She massaged the arm while I screamed, and applied liniment as I sobbed; she kneaded and stroked further, and instructed my mother to make a sling for the arm; and although she didn't charge a fee for this service, donations were of course welcome.

For days my arm hung in a dish towel that in a previous incarnation had been a Robin Hood flour bag, on which my aunt had now embroidered bananas and grapes and a bright red apple. At mealtimes I found it much easier to lower my head toward spoons and forks than to raise them to my mouth; yet pamper the arm as I would, it seemed to make no progress whatever, and one day it was determined that I should visit the clinic.

I didn't know this grandfather well, and didn't much feel like attending the Dew Drop Inn as an actual patient. But I did attend, and as Grandpa applied his arts and I barely managed to stifle new screams, he found that no further rightmaking was necessary. The arm was sprained, and we should continue as we had with the sling. "You just be brave, Lloydie," he said.

A couple of weeks later I accompanied my parents on a shopping trip to Rosthern. The sprained arm had stubbornly refused to mend, and we stopped at Friesen's Store to see an acquaintance who worked there in the furniture department, who was also a bit of a rightmaker on the side. But this man had barely touched my arm — I remember there was no pain — before telling my parents clearly that it was broken and I should be taken to the doctor at once.

I imagined the hospital visit would be short, maybe a little longer than a trip to a rightmaker. The X-rays showed two broken bones in my arm — that much they told me. But no one mentioned that the bones had grown back together, and would have to be re-broken and set properly.

By now it was evening. A nurse took me to a room at the far end of the hospital and told me to get into some pyjamas, and left. A few minutes later she returned and put me to bed. I inquired after my parents, and she said they had gone home. Then I started to bawl, but the louder I wailed, the sterner and taller the nurse grew, until her face was more frightening even than my parents' absence, and all that was left was to turn toward the bedrail and pull up the covers and beseech heaven, Now I lay me down to sleep, I pray thee Lord my soul to keep.

The next day I was wheeled into the operating room. Doctor Jack Janzen was as friendly as the nurse had been forbidding, and he bantered with me as he demonstrated his ether-dispensing apparatus. He held the mask over my nose and asked me to count to ten. By the time I got to six I was giggling, because the drowsiness made everything so very effortful, and by seven I had given up. I woke up in my room more nauseous than I had ever felt before, but amazed that I'd been put to sleep so quickly and had the bad arm fixed without any more pain. It was almost as good as a miracle.

Now I sported a cast from shoulder to wrist, with a brace forming a tiny equilateral triangle at the elbow. My parents visited a couple of times, and after a few days I went home.

The doctor's fee was forty dollars, a steep price for my parents at the time.

Back in school, it was Rosa who first noticed how hard the cast felt, and I soon discovered that it could also be used as a weapon. I brandished it fiercely at real and imaginary persons who thwarted me, and with each success at making an antagonist retreat, I waxed in power. All my friends autographed it, including some who hadn't been friends before; and when Big Ears himself printed his name, all hostilities between us were over.

In June my report card read: "Lloyd missed the final examination because of a broken arm. He is very highly recommended. (Signed) R.E." The jealousy in the second grade class went a long way in compensation for the pain — and then for the itch as the arm finally began to heal.

Our new teacher in grade three had less empathy. Where R.E. had exempted me from final exams, B.B.'s first report gave me a "U" for Unsatisfactory in Handwriting, which had suddenly been afflicted with acute left-handedness. One evening my parents invited her for supper. We sat at the living room table where we never ate unless we had guests, and I drank a glass of milk, which I hated, to prove to B.B. that we followed the Canada Food Guide or something.

Let's hope medicare stays with us awhile longer. But if not, once in awhile there is a rightmaker who knows what he's doing. Wherever you are, Henry Driedger, thanks for noticing that I had a broken arm.

TWO FATHERS, A HALF-DOZEN MOTHS

*M*Y FATHER WAS A CANADIAN PRAIRIE FARMER for most of his life. In his last ten years he was in and out of hospitals. Two heart attacks had damaged him severely, and the complications attending this, added to the sundry infirmities of advancing age, made hospital stays common for him and visits there routine for me.

"What does it mean," he asked as he lay in intensive care for the first time, "if I dream it's late autumn and the crop is in, and I remember there's one field I forgot to harvest?" This dream, which began there, re-visited him thirty or forty times in the last decade of his life, and it always ended in frustration as he found his dream-machinery broken down, and his dream-self too embarrassed to ask the neighbours for help. Yet he told me about it faithfully every time the dream recurred.

At first I supposed he wanted me to answer him. But our discussions always concluded with his indifference to any insight I thought I had contributed. To me it was patently clear — didn't Jung say that what we have woven by day the night will unravel — but not until the dozenth-or-so time did I have the sense to leave him with his own question. To his usual "So what do you think it means?" I for once replied, "I give up, Dad; what do *you* think it means?"

He fidgeted and hung his head with a grin, and said, "I guess it means there's something I've left undone." I professed not to know what it might be, and only wondered aloud *who* was telling him he had left this thing undone?

The dream kept repeating itself until his last hospitalization. Visiting him again one day, I thought he looked well, even handsome, and wore his seventy-five years so much better than many of the withered bodies along the wards of that sterile institution. He was there because of a small problem having nothing to do with his frail and swollen heart, and I couldn't have guessed I would not see him again. We had grown closer these last years, he coming to accept that his only son had taken a disorderly leave of church and marriage, I gradually learning not to explain and not to complain.

As I left the hospital that day, my hand already on the doorknob, he said, "I had that dream again, but this time I was starting to harvest the last field."

"Good for you, Dad," I said, "I'm glad to hear it." And I contented myself as I drove off that something new was in the making.

A few days later the last of the harvest was in. I was led from a waiting room, past an office and along a corridor, through a garage where a hearse waited, and into a back room where my father lay on a stark wooden table. The bruises on his head hadn't yet been masked by cosmetics; he had injured himself when his heart took him down for the last time, though the doctor tried to assure us that he never felt the blow. The undertaker excused himself and closed the door circumspectly behind him; and there, by myself, I attended to matters which do not concern others.

Confucius said that a man's character cannot be judged until after his father is dead. I had pondered this for years, supposing I understood intellectually what he meant, but fearing there was something in store which I couldn't know until my own father had died. I imagined Confucius to have foreseen something which depth psychology would lay bare to a resistant public centuries later — that we all bury so many impulses in hopes of gaining our parents' approval, that only when they are dead can those energies rise more surely toward the surface.

Of course this is true. But now I think old K'ung Fu Tzu was talking about the shadows of mortality which grow duskier in a man's mind when his father has stepped off the top rung of the ladder, and made room there for his son — and the son begins to understand that his turn is next.

I inherited a few of my father's possessions. His favourite coffee mug, his razor, a pair of slippers my mother had knit for him which he liked to wear as he sat in his chair reading, these simple things I kept in his honour. The slippers, I suppose, had been a too-emotional remembrance for my mother to endure with every opening of her bedroom closet, so she had given them to me. They lay in a dark corner of my own closet for some weeks before I took them out one early summer day and set them on the kitchen counter, thinking to wear them later that evening. They looked homely, and I had a fleeting image of my father sitting in his chair with a book, warmed by these slippers, making good in his declining years a life of prairie labour where there had been so little time to read.

I had no pressing work to do that day, and by mid-afternoon had begun celebrating my leisure with a couple of snifters of the imported brandy of which, I didn't yet like to admit, I had been growing rather too fond, sometimes letting its anaesthetic properties supplant its medicinal ones. There had been enough middle-age losses — a marriage, a religious vocation, the favour of a large extended family still in the grip of their fundamentalism, a fond conceit of being a good father to my own children, and several dear friends to cancer. Now my father, too.

I washed and dried some dishes and set them on the counter. By and by I put them away in the cupboards, and my eyes fell again on the slippers. I picked them up and a dozen dark wings flew toward the window, where I heard them beating on the glass with such urgency that I hardly knew what had just happened. The little moths had been sleeping in my father's slippers, for miles and days lain dormant in a dark woollen world where, for all I know, they might have been content to stay — had I not startled them toward the light — until the slippers had, strand by strand, become moth.

I don't know anyone who likes moths. That sickening smell of mothballs in trunks and closets which their stealthy invasion of human dwellings requires, their irritating flapping and fluttering, their being such poor cousins of the butterflies everybody loves, all this had left me indisposed toward these pathetic creatures, and yet there was something about them now...

Maybe I'd had enough of death. Maybe it was some dim science of the frailty of all existence — for how was it possible that this body of my father's should be so full of warmth and certainty at one moment, so vacant and removed at the next? Or perhaps the brandy was behaving medicinally again, making me glad there had been *some* sort of life inhabiting those forsaken slippers; or maybe it was the moths' anxious longings toward the light.

I pulled on the slippers and they carried me to the window where the night-creatures beat so frantically toward the day. I saw that I, too, am such an ambiguous creature, with inclinations toward the dark and deep, yet crying out in spite of myself *More light!* I wanted to help the moths through that invisible barrier between their unfastened instincts and the sunshine toward which they strained — no more death, not then, not if I could help it. They didn't appreciate my hands pursuing them up and down the glass as they crawled away, or the firmness with which I grasped them one by one in the windows' far corners. I forgave them their intended consumption of my Dad's slippers, carried them to the patio and turned them out to the light, and watched them flutter off toward Diefenbaker Park. The last one was the most fugitive, eluding me until it was exhausted, and when I opened my hand at the door, it sat in resignation until I nudged it into flight.

"I caught you to release you," I said, and turned and poured a redundant brandy, but that would be another story.

Is there something more high-flown to be said? I only wanted to report that a few moths had slumbered in one father's slippers, until another father turned them over to the light. Now sometimes I catch myself asking Dad, "So what does it all mean?" And I hear a familiar chuckle in his voice as he replies, "I give up, Son; what do you think it means?"

DER SCHOENER MANN

*F*OR MUCH OF MY YOUNG LIFE, Grandpa Karl Gliege was my best friend. One of my first memories is of being carried in his arms at nightfall as he sang *Gute Nacht, gute Nacht, wieder ist ein Tag vollbracht*: Good night, good night, again day takes its flight. I remember riding a train with him the ten miles from Laird to Carlton and back — steam locomotive ahead, coal car, a few boxcars, a single passenger car and caboose behind. I remember him sitting in the doorway of his workshop whittling in the afternoon sun, and calling me to him; how the thick nail of his index finger coaxed a quarter from the *Geldbeutel* that appeared from his overalls so I could get two Pepsis for us from the store, the leftover nickel buying me a Jersey Milk chocolate bar — always a Jersey Milk. I remember the buffalo hide hanging over the rafters of the car shed, left over from the days of covered sleighs. Grandpa had built seventy-eight sleighs in his workshop by the time he retired.

He died on the week I finished high school. I lay in bed that night and implored God to say hello to him from me.

When Grandpa wore his black three-piece suit, the suit in which he was buried, I thought he looked aristocratic.

But when he stood in his vast garden in spring and burned off the chicken shit he and I had hauled there on winter Saturdays, he was a simple rustic. One year he burned his manure as a powerful west wind blew smoke across the schoolyard a few steps over, where we were playing soccer and I was hoping to impress the girls watching at the sidelines. "Jeez, Giggly Gliege," Ronny Tobin snorted, all of us choking and half-blind in the smoke, and I wondered why Grandpa couldn't have waited till school was out.

He never believed humans would get to the moon. How could people think that, he asked me, when the moon is there sometimes, and other times only half there, or gone altogether? But then, I didn't believe him either when he said Berlin was so big that you could drive fifty miles from Laird to Hepburn to Saskatoon and it would all still be Berlin.

I loved sleeping over at Grandpa's house. While Aunt Anne read me bedtime stories from *The Family Herald*, I could hear Grandpa praying aloud in the room below, kneeling beside his bed near the dark wardrobe telling God his wishes — the most urgent of which was the redemption of a wayward daughter, and two black-sheep sons who hadn't given up *Tabak* as he had. Yet sometimes I thought he hadn't quite converted to Mennonitism after all; he was very fond of the Apocrypha between the testaments of his Martin Luther *Bibel*, and sometimes there was a crock of wine in the gray cupboard in the cellar, beside the cases of Peter Fahrney's *Alpenkraueter* which he sold as patent medicine — which only late in life did I discover contained a good stiff kick of alcohol.

Beside the living room door, under his old clock, stood a desk Grandpa had built. But he never seemed to sit there;

he preferred his rocking chair beside the oil stove. A few years before he died, knowing how much I liked that desk, he promised it to me if I would read through the entire New Testament in German. It was a bribe, and I took it.

And I did try to read. But weeks later, and still only a few pages in, the text began to rankle. The old German script looked like hieroglyphics, and when I had deciphered them I still had no idea what half of the words meant. So I began to cheat. Over the next week I skimmed a few chapters. By the end of another month I was flipping through good-sized chunks of gospels and epistles, and this continued, with intermittent spells of honest effort (I didn't want to be done *too* quickly) until I came at last to the Book of Revelation. I notified Grandpa that I was nearly done, and an idea came to him: why not read that last book together?

For several evenings we sat by the stove and took turns reading aloud from the *Offenbarung Johannis* — which wasn't nearly as hard as understanding it — and when Grandpa pronounced *Die Gnade unsers Herrn Jesu Christi sei mit euch allen! Amen*, and closed his Bible, the ordeal was over. He gave me the desk promptly, and for himself built another one which I thought looked shabby by comparison with mine.

But when the revival preacher from Nebraska came around, the guilt drove me back to read every bitter German page from the middle of St. Mark to the end of St. Jude, though I never did confess this to Grandpa. But I used his desk more than he ever did.

Grandpa visits me often in the night. In some dreams, I realize with a start that I haven't seen him in a very long time; I'm bewildered that I could have forgotten him, and feel deeply ashamed as I wake up. In one dream, he phones and urges me not to neglect old people: "When you need someone, turn to me," he says. Sometimes I try to talk with him, struggling toward the German words but not quite getting there, and waking up in frustration. In my best dreams of Grandpa, I fall on him overjoyed and blurt out, *Ach, du schoener Mann!* — ah, you dear man.

Grandpa's first hospitalization was also his last. He held out as long as he possibly could, but one day the *Alpenkraueter* no longer helped, and he asked to be taken to the doctor — the sooner the better, he said, *je eher je lieber*. Within a few days he was no longer able to speak. The last time I saw him, his sunken cheeks frightened me, and I had never seen such a strange, baleful look in his eyes. He gestured that he wanted to be alone with me. I felt awkward, yet very proud that he would wave two of his own daughters and another grandson from the room to be with me. They left. He tried to speak, and couldn't. I heard only dreadful, gurgling sounds in his throat. I don't know whether I touched his hand. I wish I had said, in words, that I loved him. It's unfinished business.

Good night, Grandpa, good night. Again a soul takes its flight.

Ach, du schoener Mann.

d

THE CHAMPION

*F*IRST LET ME GET THE DEVILRY OUT OF THE WAY. He was a formidable six-year-old obstacle, a runny-nosed waif with dark, suspicious eyes and something weasel-like in his face, who drove his first-grade teacher to distraction. He whined and snarled, he pestered and annoyed, he fought and he lied. Many times a day he flopped out of his desk and crawled on the floor among the legs of kids who were working obediently. He picked his nose and rolled the snot into a ball and flicked it at the teacher, then sat silently as she disintegrated, looking up through big eyes from under a growth of wiry unkempt hair. He fantasized excessively, or lied (often nobody knew which), he ate erasers, he threw things around the room and tantrums at the teacher. And once in awhile he worked a little.

There was more; but let's just say he was an impedance to the flow of all educational currents. He was so exceptional at so young an age, that no official labels had yet been hung on him — TMH, ADHD, LD, BD, ED, and no DSM diagnosis either. He was Kent (an invented name), an exception to many rules, somewhere out near the first or ninety-ninth percentile of things, and something in me found that appealing.

He's never left me alone since I met him twenty years ago. I was reeling then from the emotional batterings of my domestic separation and religious upheaval, living alone in a back bedroom of an unfinished basement in the house of some friends who had taken me in. On many a day, driving to school already felt like a day's work, and when I arrived, there was Kent, this most conspicuous of challenges — or threats — to my therapeutic skill. My years as a minister and counsellor hadn't involved much work with children, and here was a staff of educators — fresh, seasoned, or jaded — looking on to see how this newcomer would earn his keep.

With the students in university and high school, and with the adults in my four parishes, counselling had been a largely verbal and cognitive endeavour, where emotions were labelled and expressed, philosophies of life aired and inspected, messes made serviceable and hopeful through the power of words. I had been told I was a pretty good counsellor, and sometimes I half-believed it myself.

But this is not a story about skill in child psychotherapy. I had none. I had no more idea what to do with Kent, or other children, than any reasonably alert parent or teacher would have. I had played with my daughters in their childhood, and in graduate school I once had a few practicum sessions of play therapy with a mute and severely autistic girl, where my professor said I shouldn't expect anything to happen, and nothing happened. That was the extent of my expertise.

My ego had vested interests, after its recent humiliation, in demonstrating some new competence, and here among institutional outcries for corrections and remedies, it would be given a chance. They told me then I was the only full-time resident elementary school counsellor in Saskatchewan, hired in a pilot project as one of several measures taken to keep the lid on the "seething pot" the school had become. Among its seven-hundred students were many disturbed and disturbing ones, and there was an endless stream of them — their families were so transient that some years the rate of student turnover approached one hundred percent.

Since I was at a near loss in knowing how to begin under these circumstances, there was nothing to do but abandon myself to the process, trusting what I claimed to believe about the power of the life-energy bound up in these little souls. My office was a temporarily vacant classroom at the far end of a long hall, and I stocked it with the kinds of supplies to be found in any school workroom: paper, paints, clay, chalk, scissors and staplers, a few castoff posters. My furnishings were a low table and small chairs. I was given a few days to orient myself, then the sessions began.

I picked Kent up at his class that day and started the long trek to my room at the other end of the school. He followed suspiciously. When we arrived, he stood surveying the place.

"What's this?" he asked in a whining voice, pointing at some paper.

"It's paper," I said.

"What's this?"

"Paints and paint brushes."

"What's that?"

"Playdough."

He picked up a stapler. "What's this?"

"It's a stapler."

Back to the paper: "What's that?"

"Paper."

On and on, these questions.

When he had satisfied himself as to the ontology and phenomenology of each thing, I said, "We can paint or draw or talk, or play with the playdough, or whatever you like."

We sat down at the table and he surveyed the supplies at length, stared at me with great wordless eyes, and looked around the room again.

Eventually I began drawing something on a sheet of paper, mainly to hide my own discomfort. The trouble was, I had never drawn anything in thirty years, since Lyle Sawatzky in the third grade got a John Gnagy Learn-to-Draw Kit, and drew '57 Fords so dexterously that I knew at once he was an artist and I never would be. Now I had to expose to Kent that, although I had offered to draw with him, I really had no idea how to do it. I started by making a simple name tag in balloon letters which he could hang in his room at home.

Like a little tomcat he watched everything I did. The conversation was mighty sparse, and when he did reply to my questions I had no idea whether he was telling the truth anyway. I don't know how I survived that session, but at the end Kent claimed he'd like to come and visit another time.

When I fetched him again the next week, we stopped in the supply room and I said he could pick out something he liked. He stood a long while appraising what I now know must have seemed a prodigious wealth there before his eyes.

Finally he pointed at a pile of coloured paper. "Can we supply some of that?" he asked.

I said yes, and took down a few sheets.

He slowly surveyed the shelves again, then pointed at paper of a different colour. "Can we supply some of that kind?"

"Yes, we can supply that too."

He supplied a little of four or five colours; then, because I didn't know much about the paper budget, I suggested we go. As we walked the long hallway, the questions began again.

"Do you know that boy?" he asked when I said hi to someone in passing.

"Yes, I do."

"Does he know you?"

"Yes."

"Who else are you picking up today? Why?" The questions were asked in the same whining, pleading tone I had heard before, and which his teacher heard regularly when he wasn't snarling.

In my room he stood and looked around again. Things were different; a new inventory had to be taken.

"Who drew that picture? What's this? What's that? Why did you get more clay? How did you do this?" The questions either had obvious answers — "What's this?" (A paint brush); or they had no answers at all — "How did you draw that picture?" (I don't know, it just sort of came out). Many of them were the same things he had asked the previous week. This interrogation seemed to betray some huge and diffuse anxiety, though of course there was no point in saying this to him. We painted again, he filling one sheet after another with scribbles, I hunched over the table trying to produce something that would resemble a picture at all.

The principal was spending seventy or eighty percent of his time dealing with disciplinary problems, and if someone were to ask what I was doing with Kent, I'd say, "Well, we're drawing pictures — trust me, you can trust the process."

Right.

It was easy to see Kent needed stability and reassurance, and that he wanted to feel important. Besides his endless whining questions, he now began physically attacking some of his classmates whom I was seeing, too. He told outrageous stories while growing ever more emphatic that they were true. And as the weeks went on, more and more champion-talk began coming out of his mouth.

"I'm the champion drawer," he'd announce after executing, however carelessly, some kind of picture. "I'm the champion painter, I'm the champion stapler, I'm the champion drummer" — this when the music teacher had stored a bass drum in the room, which Kent pounded a few times and directly found himself an accomplished drummer. Or he'd roll a plain round ball of clay and say, "I'm the goodest bowling ball maker of all." One week somebody had left an old cap gun in the room. Kent immediately brandished it and said, "I'm the manager of the gun."

One day he summarized it: "I'm the champion of everything!"

Often he asked, "Am I the only one who did this, or made that, or who done so-and-so?" I had posted many other name tags in my room by now, but I never knew how this vexed him until one day he demanded that I make another one for him. It had to be bigger than all the others, he said, and he supervised me intently as I drew it.

One day as we were painting, he looked over my picture and concluded it was better than his. He asked, "Will you hang yours up and tell the other kids it's mine?" When I said I wouldn't lie, he vented hostility at everyone who had left paintings on my walls — he was mad, he said, "because they're champions too."

Our trips to the supply room yielded increasing quantities of material. Now he supplied a dozen sheets of each colour instead of four or five, and more clay and more staples, and more paints of all colours even though we already had plenty back in our room. I was feeling more at home by now, and acceded to all but his most immoderate requests, and he went on supplying himself ever more liberally. Settled into our sessions, he consumed these supplies with a gusto that bordered on greed — markers, staplers, paints, whatever, all went to satiate his enormous appetite, yet he often said he had such supplies at home, only his were bigger and better than these which we had here.

As the weeks went on, we found ourselves communicating much more freely. I did what I could to make the environment safe and pleasant. I reflected his comments and actions without judgment; sometimes I made simple didactic statements about how to do certain things, or I tried to make behavioural contracts with him "so there's not so much trouble for you in school." I allowed his feelings to surface and be expressed in any way he saw fit. Though I was prepared to set limits to this, and had to do so with a few others, Kent never came close to expressing emotion in a destructive way. As he warmed to me, my affection for him grew, too, and he consumed this as he did his supplies.

"How much time is left?" he often asked anxiously, checking whether he was still safe. Then he'd launch into another fantasy about how important he was. "My sister was so clumsy that she made me bump into her. Then she jumped on me and I puked all over her; then my mom came and saw it, and spanked my sister 'cause it was on purpose." "I went to Star Wars Land and saw Luke Skywalker — this ain't a story neither." "Strangers hop me in their car, but I hop out the window." "Carly said shit. I told the teacher and she gave Carly a boot in the ass." "I saw a Crystallizer that got killed and went to hell and came back to life in the hospital. It's true."

He insisted he had a real brother and a real Easter rabbit at home. He told things about invisible bugs and vampires and two-headed bathrooms. And he often had birthdays. If I pointed out that he'd just had one recently, he maintained he was having another one. "I turned seven yesterday; now I'm old enough to punch my sister in the mouth." Everything he had to say, he assured me, was true.

It wasn't his telling of these tales that worried us, but the vehemence with which he defended them; not the fabrications, but his fierce defiance of anyone's right to challenge him, especially when the stories turned into shameless lies.

But eventually another theme began to emerge, of a deepening identification with me. In one phase that went on for several weeks, he required me to do things exactly as he did — colour the same pictures in the same way, at precisely the same speed, using identical colours. He worked slowly, keeping me under surveillance and criticizing me openly when I deviated even slightly from his curriculum. "I want us to think the same," he said. "I want to be the same as you." "I want us to be twins." "You can't paint now, you have to do what I'm doing."

I was very thankful when this phase passed.

Then he began to compliment me directly. "I'm gonna stick with you." "I wish I could see you every day." Or he'd want me to compliment him: "Did you like me the first time you saw me?" "Will you like me forever?" And so on. One day he began talking about a Cheese Macro. When I said I didn't know what he meant, he explained that it was "a hamburger with a Kent and a Mr. Ratzlaff on top" — two Big Cheeses, he and I.

I knew his father wasn't with the family, yet he sometimes spoke about him as if they all lived together. His mother had explicitly denied that she was with another man, and I didn't discover till much later that she had lied — for what reason I never knew. So when Kent talked about his father, I wasn't sure how much fantasy was at work. One day he drew a picture of a vampire: "That's my dad," he said, but then qualified it, "not really — he only has two teeth. Those are my dad's claws . . . it's just a picture, 'cause I don't know what he looks like." One day he fashioned a clay figurine saying it was his dad; then he went for the stapler and shot at least a hundred staples into its head.

I soon learned that I had to give him advance notice when our sessions were nearing their end. If I waited till the bell, he'd resist with might and main leaving my room, using every trick he could invent to stay a bit longer. One day I told him we had about five minutes left. He nearly fell from his chair, but caught himself and said, "Oops, I was about to fall!"

So much for all the toppling out of his desk in the classroom.

He started playing trickster. He'd pull a little stunt, and laugh with utter hilarity when he saw he'd taken me in. "I'm a tricky little bugger," he'd say. "I joked you."

Once in awhile he wanted to do some real schoolwork, like the day he thought we should practise our printing. After we'd worked on the blackboard for some minutes, he stood back and inspected first his printing, then mine. Mine was better, he thought. He pointed at his own and said, "The Kent who wrote that died — now do you believe that?"

The Champion of Everything was passing away. Somewhere in that long subterranean process, he had blustered and plumed himself to satiety, and not until then did the grandiosity, fantasy, and jealousy abate. In the Champion's place a new little Kent began to rise. In class he demonstrated that he was quite capable of working in a sustained and co-operative way. There were stretches, sometimes several weeks in length, in which his behaviour was not only acceptable but astoundingly good; where, for instance, he'd do a half-hour's work in ten minutes, or pay the teacher unexpected and heartfelt compliments.

Sometimes the Champion reappeared for awhile, and went away, and appeared again.

There came a day when he made his first confession. "I say a lot of swears at home," he told me, "and sometimes I say the f-word at my friends so they'll leave me alone." I took this to be a test: will this guy like me if I tell the truth?

As the winter advanced toward spring, he worked through his jealousy almost entirely, and proved it at the end of a session one day. "I'd like to stay," he said wistfully, "but I know you have to visit with other kids too."

Much of the anxiety disappeared. Where once he had peppered me with his everlasting questions, now he said things that were differentiated, matter-of-fact, and emotionally articulate. "I'm scared of people I don't know." "It makes me excited when you say hi to me in the hallway." "You did that one perfect — you're a champion too!" (the old struggle, apparently, just beneath the surface). "I'm gonna try a new thing I never tried before." "I need help with this." "You're a nice man." "I said I'd do this one good — did I blow that promise?" One day he picked up a clay figure someone had left on display, and stared at it long as if thinking through something. Finally he set it down and said, "I want to make that boy happy, I won't scrunch up his clay." Another day he made an especially endearing comment. His class had played some kind of game, and when he saw me he said excitedly, "My whole team won — even me!"

Occasionally he'd sing. One of the most emotional moments of my counselling career happened one day when he had learned a new song in class. He came to my room and sang for me, *If you co-operate, you won't have to cry.* When he had finished he said, "If you forget my name, you can just sing that song and remember."

I said I didn't think I'd ever forget him.

"But maybe one time you might call me Kenneth."

I gave him a hug, and swore I would always remember him.

The nearest thing to a fight we ever had came about like this. Being so new to this work, I felt obliged to make extensive notes of my sessions with the children. I thought this would help me reflect later, or maybe help prove to my employers, if it came to that, that I was doing something useful after all, despite my frequent doubts and (I suspected) theirs. So I kept a notepad handy and jotted things down as we visited. One day Kent had had enough of this, and he gave it to me straight: "It makes me mad when you write things down!"

I said, "It's OK if you feel mad at me."

This took him aback. "How come?"

I said, "Because we're friends; people can be mad at each other and still be friends."

He thought this over for some time, then said, "If I'm mad at somebody, they don't mess with me. But you can mess with me, 'cause I care for you."

More than one fractured life was being healed.

By the time spring arrived, his snarl had softened and he was whining less and less. Often he worked with deep absorption, sent up cheers for himself when he succeeded at something, became less inclined to deny or excuse his misbehaviours in class. He was eager to share: "One for you, one for me." "We'll take turns." "We'll share this clay." And he continued to compliment me without qualification: "You're good at that." "I really like your work."

I don't want to embellish. He continued to the end of the year to frustrate the teacher more often than we'd hoped, but with this difference: now his unruly behaviours were often mingled with gestures of affection, like giving her hugs and gifts. He had to repeat the first grade.

I haven't said much about Kent's home. This is because I don't regard him as a "case", or his story as a case history, and I did as little case-conferencing about him as possible. I detest that jargon and the sterile endeavours that so often go with it. I did have a few contacts with Kent's mother, and a dozen sessions with his sister; but this is my story about him. Let me tell you one incident, though, that may fill in a few blanks.

One day as the teacher stood at the front of the room, she noticed a peculiar dark spot on Kent's eyelid. She interrupted her lesson to ask him about it, and he told the class in his then-familiar snarly tone that it was a scab from a punch he got in a fight with another kid. It sounded plausible enough.

For a couple of days he was so well-behaved that the teacher had no reason to go near him. But on the third day, standing at his desk, she saw the scab move. It was a wood tick. It had lived on his eye for three days and three nights.

The principal asked me to take him to the doctor.

I look up the meaning of the word derelict. Something has made me curious, and the dictionary has a revelation. A derelict is "something abandoned," Webster says, "specifically, a ship abandoned on high seas."

It's easy to guess why this derelict had to be a tricky little bugger, why he had to be the champion of all things, why he needed so many supplies. And I have a private opinion as to why he needed birthdays often. We come up against the ends of our capacities. We lie awake at night and wonder whether we've taken things as far as we can. Then, as Ira Progoff says, we breathe a sigh of surrender to the limits of life.

Shortly after that year, Kent and his family moved away. For some time the Department of Social Services was searching across Canada for them. I was assigned to an itinerant job, and one day about five years later I visited a school which housed a special behaviour adjustment class (as they were then known).

He saw me before I saw him, and he approached shyly. I, on the other hand, was not shy in letting him know how delighted I was to see him again. We visited till the bell summoned him back to having his behaviour adjusted, and me to a little room where I was supposed to mediate an ongoing feud between two "normal" students. But before I left that day, Kent found me again. He had painted a picture for me.

I hadn't learned much in my academic psychology about the imagery of children's drawings. In the intervening years I've acquired a greater reverence for symbol and metaphor than I had when I knew him. If I could start over with Kent, how many things I would do differently! But one reason I remain hopeful whenever I think about him — which I do often — is this picture.

An oversized yellow sun shines down on a knight emerging from a strongly-fortified castle. The castle is steel gray, and the knight appears in startling contrast, wearing an orange helmet and a green and yellow coat of mail and scabbard. He carries a blue sword in his left hand, a purple shield in his right. The shield hangs toward the earth as the knight adventures into his world, not too offensively, not too defensively, but with something that looks very much like a balance between security and quest, between risk-taking and safe-keeping. Both his armour and his shield are decorated with bright red crosses.

Who is this, if not a Champion?

HARRY ZIEGLER'S PHILOSOPHY

*Y*OU MAY NOT HAVE HEARD OF THE PHILOSOPHY of Finalism. I learned it from a little eighty-year-old Jewish man who appeared on my doorstep one day when I was pastor of the Mennonite Church in Morris, Manitoba. He was puffing and sweating and carrying two enormous duffel bags, so tired out that he just hoped he wouldn't have to break into someplace in town to sleep, but if he didn't find hospitality soon he might have to do it. And when I invited him in, he sure wished he had something to eat, so I made him a sandwich as we got acquainted.

He was Harry Ziegler, the founder of the philosophy of Finalism and the author of books about it. The books were in his bags. And no wonder he was tired — each bag must have weighed fifty or sixty pounds. He said he didn't live in any particular place, and he had no family; he travelled a circuit between Texas and Canada, staying where he could, never asking for money except when he needed a bus ticket across the border so the officials wouldn't take him for a transient. After supper I got him a motel room with money from the ministerial association's budget, and when I said goodbye, he gave me a crumpled ten-rupee note from the Imperial Bank of India, but didn't offer to show me the books.

Months later he and his bags came around again. He was about to cross the American border, maybe we'd help him with a meal and a bed, and maybe bus fare to Pembina, North Dakota. He came in and took off his shoes, and throughout the evening remained apparently oblivious to the odour. After we'd eaten, he reminded me that he was a writer. Would I like to see his books?

Certainly.

He lugged the bags to the couch, sat down, and prepared to open them. Shannon was four years old, and curious, but as she edged closer he got visibly agitated — "Back off!" he said, and waved her away — the books were coming out, this was not a business for children.

I don't know what I expected, but what he pulled out was a half-dozen school yearbooks, one for each subject on which he had written, his typed sheets pasted over photos of freshmen and volleyball teams and encouraging words from the principal. The first book concerned dentistry. Many years ago he had suffered a heart attack. He perceived a connection between this and several bad teeth he'd had at the time, for as soon as the teeth were pulled, he had recovered fully. He had, therefore, pulled all his remaining teeth as a preventive measure, and never again had his heart troubled him, even all these years later. If your teeth offend you, pull them out.

A hundred pounds of books, priced at $20 each. It was 1976. He had sold one so far.

I was especially interested in the philosophy of Finalism. This has to do, I learned, with humans extracting ores and minerals from the earth. Anybody knows that digging things out of the ground makes the earth lighter. Soon — any day now — the earth will fly out of its orbit, and that will be the end of things: Finalism. I keep warning and warning the world, he wrote, but nobody listens, so to hell with them all.

That night we gave him Shannon's room. Our new house had three bedrooms, and there was no need to tap the ministerial committee's fund.

During the night we woke to sounds of furious pacing, back and forth, back and forth — then silence. A psycho in the house after all, and kids in the next room! More pacing, more silence. Again, and longer silence. It went on for nearly an hour, until eventually we were used to it and went back to sleep.

In the morning we heard of a new book by Harry Ziegler. Inspiration had come in the night — he must be on his way now, but he knew someone with a typewriter in North Dakota, and he had an empty book in his bag for the new pages. After breakfast I dug out another old yearbook to give him against his future needs, and took him to the bus depot.

Harry came through Morris once more before we moved away. I put him up in the motel at our expense; the ministerial fund for transients had totally dried up, there were so many of them on that 75 Highway. That day he gave me a coin. It had a little hole drilled above Victoria Regina Et Imperiatrix's spiked crown. Its back was illegible; it had apparently once been worn as a pendant. Harry said he had saved nearly enough money for a ticket to Poland, his home, where he wished to go to die. He needed only to liquidate a few remaining assets for a ticket across the

Atlantic. As for his prophetic mission, those who have ears to hear, let them hear.

That Christmas there was a letter postmarked from Toronto. Under a red poinsetta on a white page was a handwritten note: "Best regards from Harry Ziegler, whom you helped out on several occasions." Harry's finally going home, I thought.

The following spring I moved to Saskatoon for graduate studies. On one of my first weeks at the university I walked past a library window, and there was Harry bent over a copy machine, his two duffel bags beside him.

I didn't go in.

From a little tin on a shelf I retrieve Harry's coin. I haven't looked at it in twenty-five years. Her Majesty is not in mint condition. With the help of bright light and a magnifying glass, I can just make out the inscription: TO COMMEMORATE THE SIXTIETH YEAR OF THE REIGN OF HER MAJESTY QUEEN VICTORIA, JUNE 1897.

No one is immune from talking nonsense, Tony de Mello said; but the great misfortune is to do it solemnly. Don't we all tote our treasured baggage around until we disappear?

I hope the founder of Finalism and Her Imperial Majesty are amused now. Finally.

BEGINNER'S MIND

In the beginner's mind there are many possibilities; in the expert's there are few.
— Shunriyu Suzuki

ONE LONG WEEKEND SOME FRIENDS AND I went to Victoria Park just before sundown to watch the fireworks. We were lucky; where the grass ends and the hill drops sharply down, we found a prime spot to spread our blankets and watch the sun setting behind the Bessborough Hotel across the river. We surveyed the people arriving, one by one, in pairs and groups, at a steady rate until there were five or six hundred of us in the park. Then came four boys about twelve years old, with a freckled toddler in grass-stained pants poking behind. We thought we were as close to the bank as anyone would care to be, but this little company squeezed by us and settled at the very edge, beside a steep path descending to the river.

We couldn't help but overhear them as we waited for the sky to darken. I was working at the time with those troubled children in a ghetto-like part of the city, accustomed to dealing with families confounded by violence, poverty, addictions, and despair, and now I found myself wishing I could work more often with the kind of innocence and alertness we saw in the faces of the group before us.

Soon they were bored. There began a vigorous spell of goofy name-calling and roughhousing. The toddler spied the downhill path and set out on an adventure, and someone went promptly to retrieve him and warn him sternly against wandering off again. But all the tomfoolery stopped short when one of them said, "Let's give away some flowers." They hopped up, and in a minute a bouquet of prairie wildflowers had appeared, and the boy who had thought of the idea set out through the park with fragrance in his fist.

I'd be skeptical myself if someone told me this story, and I don't like to believe what I saw then. He wandered among the crowd, a donor of colour and incense — hardly a cult figure soliciting money, or a bible-thumper distributing leaflets — approaching people with a surplus of generosity and asking, "Would you like some flowers?"

I wasn't surprised when a few brushed him aside; they were looking for good seats, I supposed, intent on watching the show. They were probably a bit like me, prone to casting twelve-year-olds as pranksters and troublemakers. But I could hardly believe his enthusiasm, his determination to give away the flowers, and his persistence as people rebuffed him. Old and young ones, men and women, assorted specimens of humanity going there, thinking of fireworks — and yet I doubted it, for if they had no eyes for a child offering them flowers, how did they hope to see fire in the sky? Some strode stolidly by, others glared at him in contempt, most gave him a wide berth. He approached twenty or thirty people, and every one refused him until he came back and said, "I can't do it, somebody else try."

My friends and I were quite absorbed now as we watched a second shaveling set out on his rounds, not as eagerly as the other, and with not quite the same stamina, but doing a respectable job too as he approached another dozen with the unwanted flowers, which by now were beginning to show signs of fatigue. We saw the same dreary responses, the ignoring and the ignorance, the rudeness and the blindness. He came back and said, "I can't do it either."

But a good idea doesn't die easily, especially in the mind of a twelve-year-old. Now the first kid had caught a second wind, and he, more optimistic than I, ventured into the press as cheerfully as before. And by and by there was a decent human, a young woman who looked at him with a smile and accepted the flowers.

Judging by the movement of her lips, I think she said thank you.

SILENT NIGHT

*I*T WAS JUST BEFORE CHRISTMAS. She was fourteen years old. She had left a note where her mother, but not her father, would find it, and had gone to sit on a bridge for two hours deciding whether to jump. What finally got her off the bridge, she said, was repeating doggedly to herself, "Just because my old man is an asshole doesn't mean I have to die."

When we met, one of the first things she told me was, "I used to be able to deal with my black holes by painting, but I can't even do that anymore." I had often pondered for myself the futility of repressing the death impulse, since everything that lives, dies; but I thought of what painting had meant to her, and asked, "What if you don't take the suicidal impulse literally? What if it's a symbol of an old way of life coming to an end, so something new can be created?" She replied instantly, "That's it exactly — something in my soul wants to die."

Christmas, we know, is the worst time for depressed people. The world is at a party, and they have not been invited. Many who go to the bridge don't come back. But this girl survived the holidays, and in early January we met again. She spent most of that hour talking about her schizophrenic grandmother — how the rest of the family couldn't understand her, yet she herself was a good friend of Grandma's, and the two of them had no trouble whatsoever in conversing. Then, as the bell was about to ring, she said, "But I have to tell you a dream I had the other night."

She had found herself sitting on a mountaintop, turning over a five-dollar bill in her hands, when it dawned on her that the bill was actually an envelope. From it she drew another five dollars; then a ten and several twenties, and a hundred-dollar bill — money issuing from money until it seemed there would be no end of it. She looked at the snow on the mountain, scooped up a handful, and realized she was holding a thousand tiny diamonds. Off in the distance, trees grew with golden trunks and emerald leaves, and everything in the world she could see was made of gems.

"Then I held out my arms" — she gestured for me — "and said, *I win!* And I woke up."

Two visions: drowning in black water, under ice, at the bottom of a river; sitting on top of the world, surrounded by fairy-tale wealth.

Tom Driver writes how he used to be smartly agnostic about the notion of resurrection, until one day he realized that we all come from the dead, or from nothing. He couldn't say how he started practising cell division in his mother's womb, or how he came to contract his muscles later. Nor did he know how people who had hated each other for half a lifetime suddenly found the power to embrace one another. Every initiative in life, he saw, like the appearance of a world at all, is always from nothing. If something in the soul wants to die, then something else in the soul may want to take us to a triumphant mountain and make us rich again.

A few weeks later the girl was back in that landscape, surrounded by the same wealth; but this time she was climbing the mountain. Not long after that she showed me a sketch for a new painting, of a river flowing quietly under an overhanging tree. By late spring she had enrolled in a high-school program for gifted students.

Now the dark is deep and long. The world crawls through numb days and sleeps off its frozen nights. It will bend again toward the equinox, but at Hannukah and Christmas we need the wonder of lights in the dark, gifts in the deadness of winter, silent nights for those whom the river tempts.

All is calm; all may yet be bright.

EPILOGUE
THE SOUND OF A GOING

And let it be, when thou hearest the sound of a going in the tops of the mulberry trees, that then thou shalt bestir thyself for then shall the LORD go out before thee, to smite the host of the Philistines.

— Samuel 5:24, KJV

A black butterfly lands on the blanket draped over my arm as I approach the pioneer cemetery. I'm going once more to sit in Diefenbaker Park, when the little soul stops me. I've heard that this means good luck. I've heard that psyche means both soul and butterfly, and I fancy this one has come to visit on my last walk. I've lived near this park for fifteen years, longer than anywhere else in my life, and the place has been my tutor and my therapist. I'm moving away, willing, unwilling, resigned.

Once you were a worm, I tell the soul, and look at you now. But your wingtips are frayed — and I ponder how it's only June and already things are crumbling. I whisper my thoughts about the wind and the way and the second coming, and the soul sits for a moment before flying on.

It returns later as I approach Vernon Leo Kuhn's grave, on which the chokecherry bush grows. There's the second coming, I think, and maybe it likes me. For an instant we understand each other from bottom to top and all around our frayed edges; then it flies away, and comes again a third time as I spread the blanket farther on between the trees and hedges away from the breeze.

I hear geese honking furiously north, crows making harsh racket as they shift from branch to branch, a hawk overhead crying its meaning. "When you hear the sound of a going," it was said, "God goes out before you."

Annie Dillard thinks the point of Creation is that each thing should get noticed. These goings and stirrings and soundings — the kingdom of heaven coming and coming again. God sits in a mulberry tree and sounds like a going, waves us on, smites philistines within and without, sits on our blanket and makes us notice. Luther said if he knew the second coming would happen tomorrow, he'd still weed and water his garden today.

A disciple once interrupted a Zen master who was weighing flax, and asked him, "Please tell me the meaning of life."

"This flax weighs five pounds," the master explained.

What's blasphemy but the other side of wish? Grace lands in a black butterfly, here on the midway where we find ourselves, with heaven beyond where grace isn't needed and hell opposite where none is available — here in this world, the ordinary place for grace.

This semi-circle of trees and hedges has been a sanctuary for fifteen years. Rudy Wolfe planted them thirty-seven years ago; now they're half as high as a country elevator. He tends them faithfully today, still watering, pruning, carrying away storm-tattered branches. He was alone in these trees when I first met him, and we spoke, and he went back to them when I left.

Two goldfinches flash by and lift up my heart. I feel it physically, sacramentally. A fat bumblebee comes, and other species of butterflies, many souls going.

How long have I sat here? The breeze has become a Saskatchewan wind shaking the treetops, almost like a Kansas dust storm to make one long for the emerald city. But the black butterfly landed; no wind can blow that away.

Here's the sound of my going. Thanks, Mr. Wolfe, for tending the garden when the Gardener was absent.

AUTHOR PHOTO BY LARRAINE RATZLAFF

LLOYD RATZLAFF was born and raised in Saskatchewan, and makes his living as a writer in Saskatoon.

He obtained a Bachelor of Arts degree in Psychology from the University of Winnipeg, a Bachelor of Theology from Providence College, and a Master of Education in Counselling from the University of Saskatchewan.

Both his creative non-fiction and professional pieces have been widely published throughout Canada and the United States.

Quebec, Canada
2002